# BEYOND FOO

## — Geth and the Deception of Dreams —

# BEYOND FOO

— Geth and the Deception of Dreams —

# OBERT SKYE

SHADOW
MOUNTAIN

For Bennett
By far one of the best parts of my life

Kor Mor Se Log

Visit us at ShadowMountain.com

**Library of Congress Cataloging-in-Publication Data**
Skye, Obert.
    Geth and the deception of dreams / Obert Skye.
        pages   cm — (Beyond Foo ; book 2)
    Summary: Beyond the borders of Foo lies the land of Zendor—a place where dreams are held captive with little thought for hope, but now Clover and Geth are determined to change that.
    ISBN 978-1-60908-896-5 (hardbound : alk. paper)
1. Fantasy fiction.  [1. Dreams—Fiction.  2. Magic—Fiction.
3. Voyages and travels—Fiction.]  I. Title.  II. Series: Skye, Obert.
Beyond Foo ; book 2.
    PZ7.S62877Gc 2012
    [Fic]—dc23                                                    2012023504

Printed in the United States of America
Publishers Printing, Salt Lake City, UT

10   9   8   7   6   5   4   3   2   1

# CONTENTS

# Contents

## ✦ Chapter One ✦
# TANGLED UP

The blackness cinched up its belt and forced the breath out of Geth and Clover like a pair of tight pants after a large dinner. Clover breathed out quickly through his small nose and then let air slowly seep back into his lungs. "It's so dark," he whispered. "I can barely breathe. Listen." He breathed a few deep, labored breaths to prove his point.

"You're fine," Geth insisted. "Besides, dark has nothing to do with the oxygen levels."

"Tell that to my lungs," Clover argued.

Geth held his unconscious brother, Zale, in his arms like he was some sort of spineless bride. His brother was still unconscious from the hit Geth had administered when they left the castle minutes ago.

Zale's body was small and light, the years he had spent sitting alone in prison having left him with the physique of a bony rag doll. His long, black beard was one of the weightier parts of his body. Geth shifted Zale up over his right shoulder.

"Ouch!" Clover wailed. "Your brother's limp arm slapped me."

"Blame him when he comes to," Geth said. "But for now, be quiet."

"I didn't ask to be hit," Clover pointed out.

"Quiet," Geth repeated. "There are things out here that can hit much harder than that."

It was pitch-black, but even in the dark it was easy to see that Geth's personality had become more intense than ever. Clover could hear the added strength in Geth's words and the quick, passionate way that Geth spoke. Payt's voice had fired up Geth's brain, creating drive and fight in ways that even Ezra would have been impressed by.

"I was just saying that—"

"Quiet," Geth ordered.

Geth and Clover had moved slowly through the gardens outside Pencilbottom Castle, feeling their way forward. Geth's legs were scratched and marred from all the thornbushes and walls he had hit up against, but they were making decent time despite the dark.

"I still have a glow stone," Clover reminded Geth. "We could use that to see where we're going."

"Not yet," Geth whispered. "We need to get farther from the castle. There's someone out here that I'd rather not see at the moment."

"Who?" Clover asked.

"Shhh," Geth begged.

They passed through the small wall in front of the castle heading down the cobblestone road. They were moving toward the vacant houses and shops Geth had helped set fire to the night before.

The small, empty town that surrounded Pencil-bottom Castle was called Finis. In the past it had housed hundreds, but as Payt had cruelly taken over the realm of Zendor and built a massive wall circling the town, beings had either fled or been turned into boors.

The air in Finis still smelled like smoke from the damage Geth and the Tangle had done. Geth bumped into a wooden post that had once been a streetlight. He moved around the pole, took two steps, and ran into the side of a stone wall. He lifted his arms and felt the bottom of an open window.

Geth inched his way along the side of the building.

"It smells burnt here," Clover observed.

"Seriously," Geth whispered, "it's important that you keep quiet, now more than ever."

"But it makes me hungry," Clover added softly, slow as usual to heed instruction. "Not the being quiet part, the smoke part. Besides, who's going to hear us, anyway? Nobody can see us, and that Payt guy probably thinks you were eaten by those smelly dogs."

"I'm not keeping quiet for Payt's sake," Geth said. "I'm keeping quiet because I'd like to get Zale somewhere safe before we run into . . ."

Geth stopped talking and moving.

"Honestly," Clover complained. "You have a real problem with finishing your sentences. I always have the courtesy to . . ."

Clover stopped speaking.

The sound of something moving toward them could be heard in the distance. They held their breath and opened their ears as wide as they could. Like a radio slowly being turned up, a low growl filled the air.

"What direction is that coming from?" Geth asked calmly.

"From behind you!" Clover said. "No, from in front! I can't tell!"

Geth shifted Zale to his other shoulder and stood up as tall as he could. The low growl was now accompanied by a rhythmic click of feet stamping closer.

4

"Keep invisible," Geth ordered Clover. "The last time I messed with this thing, it bested me. We'll need one of us to remain free, so keep still and quiet."

Geth stood stiffly as the noise grew louder—the Tangle was coming. There was no point in running because Geth couldn't see two inches in front of himself.

The noise grew louder and louder until the sound of heavy hooves could be heard just to the right of them. The beast stomped and snorted, sending small flecks of spit onto Geth, Clover, and Zale.

The Tangle grunted and hollered. The beast threw its tail down and hammered at the stone road violently, making it sound like they were standing in the world's darkest and most frightening destruction site.

The beast roared loudly and then moaned. Warm air from its massive lungs drifted around Geth's head. Geth kept his place, not moving at all. There was a swishing sound and the noise of something moving away. After at least a minute there was still no sound. Clover couldn't handle the silence any longer.

"What was—"

A massive roar ripped through the dark as the Tangle bellowed. The beast blew fire up into the sky and instantly lit up the scene. The Tangle had moved back, but it was still only a dozen feet away. Geth stood there with Zale over his left shoulder and an invisible sycophant on his right. Whereas most men and women might have simply passed out from fear, Geth smiled like it was Christmas and someone had just given him the gift of potential danger.

"We meet again," Geth said lustily.

The Tangle blew fire to the left and lit up the top of the wooden streetlight. The fire gave the scene a sinister, flickering glow.

"I won't be as kind as I was before," Geth warned.

The Tangle stood in front of Geth. It was a good two feet taller than the lithen, with large, curved horns that grew from the sides of its head. Its big eyes shone with pupils the size and color of silver dollars. The creature's nose and mouth jutted out, giving it a doglike snout. It had a bare chest and large arms that rippled with muscles the size of watermelons. Its massive legs were covered with fur, and it stood on two hooves as it slowly lifted its long, thick tail and swatted it down against the cobblestoned street. It looked like some sort of mythical ox-lizard-bear-dog.

As if the Tangle weren't ugly enough, things were about to get even uglier.

### ✦ Chapter Two ✦

# NOT BETTER PAYT THAN NEVER

**P**ayt stepped out from behind the beast. He was wearing a smile and a short, black robe over tights and pointed shoes. Payt had a small crown on his head and held a short scepter in his right hand. He raised the scepter up and spoke directly to the Tangle, manipulating his voice to control the beast.

"Hold still."

The Tangle grew silent and settled where it stood. The scene was quiet and serene, with nothing but the sound of fire crackling sharply in the night.

"So you escaped," Payt sneered. "Big deal. And I see you took your brother—so what? You will never make it out of here alive."

Payt had meant it to be a threat, but Geth didn't

cower. Instead, he stepped closer. Geth's blue eyes were half closed, and the right corner of his mouth twisted upward in a smile.

"If I were a wagering man, I'd bet you were wrong about that," Geth said passionately. "Of course, we lithens don't see much value in wagering. Fate knows what's coming."

"My voice will keep you still," Payt said, modulating his voice to have an effect on Geth. "Your lithen blood can't protect you. Look what I've done to your brother."

Payt's voice controlled many in Zendor, but there were some who didn't feel its power. Geth's brain had been slightly touched by it, but not in the way that Payt had wanted.

Geth moved closer to Payt.

Payt had been in Zendor for years, but he still looked like the young man who had been first snatched in. His face was clean shaven and his blond hair and green eyes gave him the appearance of a young kid dressing up and playing king. As Geth moved closer, Payt squared his shoulders and stood as tall as he could.

"You know how this works," Payt tried to reason. "It doesn't have to be difficult. You work for me, and I'll reward you in ways you never dreamed of."

"Don't mention dreams," Geth spat.

Payt flinched.

"You have no right," Geth contined. "This realm has cowered as you have captured and killed every dream you could. I'm taking my brother and will return as soon as I can to defeat you and every boor who fights with you."

Payt laughed.

"Of course, you can always just surrender now," Geth suggested. "It would save a lot of lives."

Payt laughed again. "What do I care about others' lives? This is a stupid conversation. You are one man with a crazy brother over your shoulder and some out-of-control stuffed animal, wherever he is."

Clover booed from atop Geth's left shoulder.

"You don't even belong here," Payt argued. "This isn't Foo, Geth. This is Zendor, and I rule it."

"Not for long," Geth warned.

"Yes, for longest," Payt said immaturely.

"We'll see," Geth replied calmly.

"We're already seeing," Payt cried. "You can't talk like that here in my world. You can't talk like that to me. This is my land, my kingdom, I'm king."

"Where's Eve?" Geth asked.

"My soon-to-be wife is at the castle," Payt said,

sounding small. "She made the mistake of going after you in Foo, but I will still reward her with my love."

Clover made a vomiting noise.

Geth was quiet for a moment and then spoke. "So, are you done?"

Payt stomped his feet.

"You rule over a bunch of lifeless dolts," Geth pointed out. "You're forcing Eve to marry you because if her mind were her own she would kill you herself. The rest of your subjects hide from you. Yeah, you're quite the ruler."

"Insubordinate!" Payt raged, turning to face the Tangle. "Destroy him!"

The Tangle suddenly came back alive, looking like a volcano that had just been turned on. It stamped its hooves and blew fire up into the dark night.

"Watch me rule!" Payt hollered.

Geth turned to run, but the Tangle whipped its tail around so quickly that it flicked his legs out from under him and sent him flying to the ground. Geth let go of his brother and pushed him sideways. Zale rolled over the cobblestone street and up against the side of a vacant storefront while Geth lay sprawled out on the street.

Payt stepped up to Geth.

The Tangle roared as Payt stood over Geth with a

long steel sword. The wannabe king lifted the sword above his head and stared down at Geth.

"You shouldn't make me mad," Payt yelled. "I'm addicted to getting even."

"What a stupid addiction," Geth mocked.

Payt moved to thrust the sword down, but as he did so, Clover leapt up off the ground and shot directly toward Payt. Still invisible, Clover swiped at Payt's face with his long, recently acquired claws.

Payt screamed, sounding more like the queen than the king. He dropped the sword. His face now had five deep claw marks running diagonally across it. The marks began to ooze blood. Payt yelled, waving his arms around like a fleshy windmill.

Clover jumped away and into the safety of the dark.

Geth shot back up onto his feet and barreled into the shrieking king. The two of them flew across the street and hit down against the ground with a hollow smack. Payt made a noise similar to that of a massive balloon popping and then just lay there out cold.

Geth got up and turned around just as the Tangle was reaching for him. Geth darted to the right and weaved up and around the beast. He jumped on the back of the creature, trying desperately to wound or slow the beast in any way possible.

to figure out how to work the lever and gears. The lever had six arms, requiring six people to stand behind them and push them to raise the gate. Geth shoved on one of the arms, but it didn't budge. Clover walked in and up to the lever. He tried to beat against one of the arms, but it didn't help.

"Get your friend to push," Geth instructed Clover.

Clover jumped back outside, and in a second Edgar came busting through the door like an obedient giant. Clover instructed him, and the Tangle grabbed one of the six arms and pushed.

The wood arm snapped off.

"He's too strong," Geth said with excitement.

Clover had him try pushing another arm; it broke off too.

"This isn't good," Clover said. "If Payt's awake, he'll be coming soon. And if we're still here when the light comes, we'll be caught for sure."

"I know," Geth said, waving. "Come on."

Clover threw Geth a glow stone and ordered Edgar to follow him. Geth ran out of the gatehouse and picked up Zale. Zale finally began to stir.

"What's happening?" Zale asked, confused.

"We're getting out of here," Geth replied.

Zale looked around, trying to figure out where he was and what was happening.

"I told you to leave me in my cell," he panicked. "Let me down!"

"I'm not leaving you," Geth insisted. "Now, are you going to help us out?"

"No!" Zale cried. "Payt will kill you. You won't even make it past the wall."

Edgar came crashing out of the gatehouse with Clover on his shoulder, holding a glow stone. Zale saw Edgar and screamed in such a way that even Geth was embarrassed.

"What's the deal with your brother?" Clover asked. "He doesn't exactly seem like a lithen."

Zale struggled with Geth, trying desperately to get away.

"We're not leaving without you," Geth argued.

The Tangle whipped its tail and wrapped the end of it around Zale's ankles. He yanked him up and out of Geth's arms and held him dangling above the ground. Zale batted and swung at the air like an angry piñata.

"Release me!" Zale screamed. "I demand to be returned."

"Come on," Geth said, ignoring his bother and waving at Edgar. "We're going up and over."

"The wall?" Clover asked worriedly. "How are we going to get down the other side? That's a high drop."

"We'll figure that out at the top," Geth said confidently.

"Shouldn't we figure that out down here?" Clover reasoned. "I just think that it would be the responsible—"

"Lights!" Zale yelled.

Geth turned and looked back in the direction of the abandoned town of Finis. In the far distance he could see that some of the windows in the castle lit up. There were no other lights anywhere, except for the large ball of white that was coming down the cobblestone road and heading directly toward them.

"It's Payt," Zale screamed. "You fools! He'll think I'm with you. He'll think I'm helping you."

"Quiet," Geth ordered.

"He's moving quickly," Clover yelled. "What's he riding in?"

"He's got all kinds of machines," Zale panicked. "It's probably one of his death wagons. That's what he does, he builds things that hurt or kill people. He'll kill us all."

"We've got Edgar," Clover said, motioning to the Tangle.

"Payt's voice controlled the Tangle before," Geth reminded Clover. "If he talks at him again, who knows whose side he'll take?"

Geth took his brother by the arm and pulled him toward one of the wooden ladders that were hooked to the scaffolding on the backside of the massive wall.

"No!" Zale screamed. "Leave me down here."

Without any instruction from Geth or Clover, Edgar flipped Zale around and carried him in his long arms.

"Thanks," Geth yelled as he began to climb up one of the wide ladders. "Hurry!"

Geth climbed the ladder to the first platform as fast as he could. The Tangle, with Zale in his arms, scurried behind him, breaking the wooden steps and scaffolding as he climbed. Geth moved up the next row of wood steps to the top of the wall. The entire wooden structure shook and cracked under the weight of Edgar. Geth looked down and out and could see Payt's white light drawing closer. Small flashes of orange began to appear and zip nearer.

*Pfssst.*

Flaming arrows whistled past them, sticking into pieces of the scaffolding.

Clover and Zale both screamed as if they had called each other up earlier and planned to express the same panic at the same time. Geth reached the very top of the wall and stood up in one of the openings of the sawtooth pattern of stone that ran the entire length. Edgar pounded up onto the crown of the wall as more and more burning arrows hit the scaffolding and spread large flames below them.

"What now?" Clover yelled.

Geth looked down at the burning fires and the flocks of flaming arrows that were still flying through the dark. The stairs they had just come up were now burning in earnest. Down on the ground Geth could see three strange wagons with large wheels coming to a stop. The wagons had big, burning torches on the front of them and tall platforms filled with crossbows.

"Let me go!" Zale demanded while pounding on Edgar. "You've trapped us up here and we're going to die."

"Seriously, Geth," Clover said, looking down into the darkness on the other side of the wall. "Your brother's a real downer."

A flaming arrow missed Geth by a couple of inches and flew over the wall. Geth watched it disappear into the pitch-dark.

The fire was raging directly beneath them now. Smoke filled their lungs and eyes. Geth looked down into the fields on the other side. The flames were now burning the wooden gate and sending light through the iron bars to illuminate the outside world.

"This night has ended up being much more exciting than I had anticipated," Geth said with gusto.

"You're thinking of jumping, aren't you?" Clover yelled.

"Seems like that's what fate's lined up for us," Geth said, stepping to the edge of the wall.

"Sometimes I hate fate," Clover said, still sitting on the shoulder of Edgar. "Would it kill fate to provide a slide or something?"

"This will be much more memorable," Geth said.

"You can't jump," Zale argued.

"I hate when people tell me what I can't do," Geth said, excited.

"Me too," Clover agreed.

Geth turned and leapt as far from the wall as he could.

"Follow him!" Clover ordered.

Edgar didn't hesitate for a moment, leaping from the wall and away from the fire. Zale screamed, the Tangle howled, and Clover braced himself for the impact, hoping at the very least that they would not land on Geth and, more important, that they would live to see that they hadn't.

## Chapter Four

# RUN CAREFULLY

Knowing who your true friends are is not always easy. Sure, you might think that the person you grew up with, learned to swim with, had sleepovers with, and took karate with is a true friend. But what happens when you discover that they were simply training to fight you in the middle of the night after swimming across a lake to sneak-attack you? I'll tell you what happens: you feel like a sap, and not the kind of sap that comes from a tree, but the kind of sap that people point at and make fun of for being sticky and dense.

Geth was no sap. Of course, you could argue that when he spent time in Reality as a tree, he had sap flowing through his veins, but even though that was true, he was far from being a sap at the moment. He knew that fate would not fail him, but he had no idea that fate would also point out who his friends really were. Zendor had been one wild ride that he had not voluntarily stood in line to get onto. But, being the lithen and all-around good person he was, Geth was holding his arms up and screaming the whole way. He might not have asked for the ride, but he was going to enjoy taking it.

Geth flew through the air toward the ground. He held the glow stone in his right hand and tried to keep his feet down in front of him. Right before hitting the soil, he was caught by some sort of material, and he rolled against the ground without a scratch. The glow stone flew from his hand. Before he could even begin to figure out what had happened, Edgar crashed down directly beside him.

Clover managed to keep hold of his stone as Edgar stumbled and held onto Zale. The great beast stayed upright and kept running forward on his massive legs. Geth moved out of his way and grabbed the tail as he shot by.

"Keep running!" Geth yelled up to Clover.

They tore through fields of tall witt that grew like thick stalks of super corn. Edgar got his stride and continued to run with Zale in his arms and Geth in his tail. They moved deeper and deeper into the fields without slowing.

"Hide your stone!" Geth yelled to Clover. "Turn off the light but keep running."

Clover pocketed the stone in his void, and everything went dark. Edgar ran for a couple hundred more yards and then began to slow.

"This—" Zale started to speak.

"Quiet," Geth ordered.

Zale reluctantly held his tongue. In the far distance they could all see the long line of orange flames as the fire they had escaped rose up over the top edge of the great wall and shone through the iron gate.

"Are you okay?" Geth whispered, figuring that they were far enough away to talk.

"Fine," Clover said. "The jump was no problem for Edgar. Did you see that machine Payt was driving?"

"I did," Geth answered as Edgar continued to run. "He likes to build things."

"I can't believe we actually made it out," Clover said proudly. "I'm going to smell like smoke for days."

"Would you two stop talking?" Zale demanded as he held his hands up over his ears. "My mind is spinning."

Clover stared at Zale from the top of Edgar's head. He looked back at Geth.

"Your brother really is great," Clover mocked. "It would have been a shame if he had hurt himself jumping. Hey, how come you didn't get hurt?"

"Something broke my fall," Geth answered.

"Something?"

"I think it might have been those girls I met earlier."

"Girls?" Clover questioned.

"I met them yesterday," Geth said. "They helped me get over that wall in the first place."

"Is that what you're going to tell Phoebe?" Clover asked condescendingly. "'Cause you might want to think up something more believable."

"That's what happened," Geth replied.

"Still," Clover whispered back. "I think long, complicated lies are much easier to swallow."

"I think you're annoying," Zale insisted.

"See," Clover said, "that's too simple. Nobody's going to believe that."

"Let's keep moving," Geth said, hoping to distract everyone from the conversation. "And let's move more cautiously. The trail we've left so far will be easy to follow if they find it."

They jogged carefully through the tall stalks. It wasn't easy for Edgar, but he was surprisingly nimble for such a big beast, especially since he still had to carry Zale. After a couple of miles and some creative turning and maneuvering, they stopped in a thick field and tramped down a spot to rest.

It was dark, but Geth could hear Edgar shiver and let out a soft bellow. The Tangle released Zale and lay down on the ground.

"I think he's tired," Clover informed Geth.

"We should be okay here," Geth said.

"So we can sleep?" Clover asked hopefully.

"For a little while," Geth replied. "At least until the light comes."

"This realm is way too dark," Clover complained. He then yawned and lay down next to Edgar.

"This realm will be the death of you both," Zale said loudly and more to himself than anyone else. "I'm already wishing I had been born an only child."

"I'm glad you're alive too," Geth said, shaking his head.

"Really?" Clover questioned.

"Could you just be quiet for a few minutes," Zale complained. "This is way more noise than I'm accustomed to."

Geth and Clover weren't necessarily in the mood to be accommodating to Zale, but seeing how they were all tired, nobody replied, and sleep quietly overcame all of them.

## + Chapter Five +

# CHILDREN OF THE TORN

Sleep is such a miraculous thing. Who in their right mind doesn't enjoy closing their eyes and getting forty winks? Of course, who in their right mind doesn't enjoy receiving forty winks with their eyes open? A wink can mean a lot of things. I've personally seen a wink mean, *Nice work, sailor, we're proud of you.* I've also seen it mean, *I saw you take that last harpoon gun and I won't tell a soul.* I've even seen it mean, *Wait ten seconds for the coast to be clear and then run as fast as you can before the guards begin shooting and you end up sleeping with the fishes.* The point is, non-fishy sleeping is really dreamy sometimes. There's nothing like letting your brain exhale and having dreams come rushing in to occupy your gray matter. Sleep and its first cousin

Dreams are two of the best gifts that we as humans can enjoy. And, not to make you jealous, but sleep and dreams are even more rewarding and more intense in Zendor and Foo than here in Reality. Yep, there's nothing like dreaming in a place where dreams can actually become whole.

Okay, that was something that needed to be said. Hopefully you didn't fall asleep. If you did, let's hope you're dreaming.

The dreams Geth and Clover had as they lay there hidden in the fields of Zendor were beautiful. Geth dreamt about his family and Phoebe, while Clover dreamt of candy and Lilly. In fact, Clover was dreaming about being beautifully caught up in a web of Fairy Floss when he woke up and realized that sometimes dreaming can be a distraction that leaves you vulnerable and open for capture.

Clover was the first of the four to wake up. He tried to stir and stretch, but his arms and legs were strapped down to the ground by hundreds of strands of string. He was pinned to the soil between the tall stalks of purple vegetation. His head was also held to the ground by bands of string across his forehead. He couldn't move anything besides his eyes and mouth.

"Um, Geth," Clover whispered, unable to turn his head. "Are you there?"

"Right here," Geth whispered back.

"Are you tied up?"

"Yes," Geth answered.

"Did your brother do this?"

"If he did, he also tied up himself," Geth replied. "I can see him to the side of me. Edgar's also strapped down. Can you move at all?"

"Nope," Clover answered.

"Neither can I," Geth said calmly. "I can barely blink."

Geth and Clover struggled with their bands for a few moments, but there was no budge or give in the least.

"It's a dirty move tying someone up when they're sleeping," Clover criticized. "I'd like to see them tie me up to my face."

"Hello, Geth," a voice from above them called out.

Geth stared up and saw Anna's face move into view as she looked straight down at him. Strands of her light red hair hung like springs, and she appeared more curious than upset.

"Anna," Geth said.

Anna smiled, happy that Geth had remembered her name.

"Did you do this?" Geth asked. "Tie us up?"

"We did," she replied.

"You did an amazing job," Geth complimented. "I can't move an inch."

Anna blushed.

"Were you outside the wall last night?" Geth asked.

"We were," Anna answered. "We saw the flames behind the wall, and while investigating, we saw you silhouetted up on the wall. When you came flying down, we did what we could to break your fall."

"Thanks," Geth said.

"You're welcome," she said dryly.

"So, do you think you could untie us?"

"Not without some answers," she replied. "For starters, what is that thing?" Anna pointed in the direction of the Tangle.

"That's Edgar," Geth replied. "He's a Tangle, and he's with us now."

"He's very impressive," Anna said, shivering. "But not impressive in the same way you are."

"Hey, Geth," Clover called out. "Tell her about Phoebe."

"And what's that thing?" Anna asked.

"That's Clover," Geth answered. "He came from Foo with me and Eve."

"He looks like trouble," Anna observed. "He has very suspicious features."

"I can hear you," Clover said.

"Clover's the one who has tamed the Tangle," Geth told her. "The big beast seems mesmerized by him."

"So who's the other bearded person?" Anna asked.

"My brother, Zale," Geth answered.

Geth could hear the sound of anxious and excited whispering all around him. Anna's eyes widened and her head shook in bewilderment.

"The lithen?" she asked.

Geth tried to nod but couldn't. "Yes."

"Eve was right," Anna said reflectively.

"Yes," Geth said with excitement. "And Eve is still alive. Payt has her."

"Then she won't be alive for long," Anna said sadly. "We've been over this before, Geth. Nobody lives if Payt has promised they'll die."

"Look at us," Geth reasoned. "We made it in and out of the castle when you said it was impossible."

"It was," Anna insisted.

"I find that hard to believe, seeing as how we're alive," Geth said, laughing. "We've even brought out Edgar."

"The beast is magnificent," Anna admitted. "And if you really can control him, that's impressive."

"Clover controls him," Geth told her. "But we can now use him and all of you to capture the castle and put an end to Payt."

"I want to believe you," Anna said. "But Payt won't lose. He has already begun to tear up the landscape looking for you. Boors are wandering deeper into fields this morning, and some are burning crops and tearing apart hills in hopes of finding you."

"Then you have to untie us," Geth insisted. "Payt has to be stopped."

Anna pulled back, and Geth could no longer see her face above him. There was nothing but clear purple sky. Geth heard some whispering, and after a few minutes Anna's and three other girls' heads slid into view above him. One girl had blonde hair, one had brown, and the other had black.

"We're not sure what to do with you," Anna admitted. "The suggestions are rather varied."

"I say we keep him tied up so that he doesn't leave us," the black-haired girl said.

"I'd be willing to watch him," the blonde one offered.

"Oh, no," the brown haired one argued. "*I'm* watching him."

"Quiet," Anna said, embarrassed. She looked at Geth's blue eyes and tried not to sound weak. "We never should have helped you up over that wall."

"I disagree," Geth said.

"We were foolish to get involved."

"That's not true."

40

"Now look at you," Anna said as all four girls took a good look at him. "This is trouble. If we release you, you'll beg us to help. I admit that it's interesting you made it in and out of there alive. I also admit that I am intrigued by the beast you have conquered. And we are all most curious about your brother."

"Leave me out of this," Zale spoke up.

Anna glanced in Zale's direction and then moved her eyes to look back down at Geth.

"Eve spoke of you and your brother changing things," Anna said. "She said that we would be able to walk free. That'd we'd no longer be Those Who Hide."

"That will happen," Geth assured Anna.

"We didn't believe her," Anna said honestly. "We still don't."

The black-haired girl leaned down farther, as if to kiss Geth.

"What are you doing?" Anna said frantically.

"I thought maybe it would help if I kissed him," the girl tried to explain.

"No," the blonde one insisted. "I think maybe I should."

Anna reprimanded them both as the brown-haired one leaned down and quickly kissed Geth on his bound nose. Anna pulled all of them away, and once again Geth could see only purple sky. After a long bout of harsh whispering, Anna's face reappeared.

"Sorry about that," she said coolly.

"Will you let us go?" Geth said, unfazed by what had happened.

"Payt's been looking for you all morning," Anna restated. "As soon as it was light, his servants worked their way out of the burnt gate, and they've been patrolling the main road in droves. You'll be caught sooner or later. Your beast left a pretty good trail through the stalks. Lucky for you the boors who serve Payt are idiots."

"Please," Geth urged, "untie us. We have to put a stop to this."

"You'll fail," Anna said.

"Thanks," Geth replied. "You've made that perfectly clear a couple of times."

"I'm just trying to manage expectations," Anna said. "You think if we untie you, that means things are going as they should. Well, you're wrong. Us untying you is just us helping you to your demise."

"Geez," Clover complained from his spot on the ground. "She's as depressing as your brother."

Anna pulled back so that, once more, all Geth could see was the purple sky. He could hear more whispering, followed by the sound of bands snapping loose. Geth felt his right arm come free from the soil.

Seconds later his left arm and both his legs were unbound. The straps against his chest loosened, and his head was finally released. Geth breathed in as deeply as he could and then exhaled. Two of the girls helped him sit up and began to rub his shoulders and arms. All the women were a bit dusty, and their clothes were torn, a natural side effect of their living in the fields.

"Thanks," Geth said. "I'm fine."

Geth was tall and strong. He had long, dusty-blond hair and blue eyes that were as deep and complex as any clear lake or open sky. In the past, optimism had been his entire personality, but now, with some of the changes that had been forced upon him, he was not only growing fiercer, he was also discovering the capacity to feel sorrow and all its depths. The new emotions were wreaking havoc on his once perfectly hopeful personality. Geth had also been without a shirt since Payt had captured him, and as he sat there with a host of ballerinas and female doctors staring at him, he felt a bit underdressed.

"Are you okay?" the dark-haired girl asked coyly.

"He looks really good," a girl dressed as an athlete said dreamily.

"I could use a shirt," Geth said.

"Here," Anna said with little emotion. "I thought you might need this."

The girls around Anna moaned in disapproval, preferring that Geth go shirtless. Geth took a white bit of cloth from Anna and unfolded it. It was a T-shirt that was at least three sizes too small. He slipped the tight shirt over his head and pulled it down. The girls who had disapproved were happy with the fit.

Geth glanced around. He could see Clover pinned to the ground. Zale was tied down and moaning, and Edgar was wrapped so tightly to the ground that the only part of him Geth could see was a bit of his dark nose and some of his right eye and horns. Geth watched the big beast's bands tremble in vain as it tried to pull up and out of the cords. "Could you let me out?" Clover complained.

Geth moved to help Clover, but he was stopped by Anna.

"Not yet," she instructed. "We're still not sure that you're not going to harm us."

Geth stood up and pushed back his long hair—a number of the women ohhhed and ahhhed.

"Listen," Geth said nicely, "the only person I want to harm is Payt. I plan to gather as many people who will fight with me."

"You don't understand," Anna argued while flexing her feet and standing on her toes. "You're too stubborn to realize that nobody here will fight. Payt's voice will

44

steal the soul of everyone and the little bit of freedom we have will be nothing but a memory. We've seen it happen hundreds of times. Like Lars has said, our best strategy is to wait."

"Lars," Zale said with interest.

"Who's Lars?" Geth questioned.

"He's quite wise," Anna said seriously. "You would do well to speak to him."

A woman dressed in a business suit and one dressed like a nurse came running out of the tall purple stalks. They were breathless and their faces were red from excitement.

"They've found the trail," the nurse said. "They're coming."

Anna looked at Geth with panic in her eyes.

"They'll be here quickly," the businesswoman said.

"Everyone scatter!" Anna ordered. "Hide until you are sure of your safety."

Geth scrambled over to Clover and began to untie him.

"You can't outrun Payt," Anna argued.

"Untie my brother," Geth ordered.

"I'm not going with you," Zale yelled. "Leave me."

Anna began untying Zale as he yelled at her. She stared at the lithen, looking confused.

"You're the one Eve said would save us?" she asked in disbelief.

"I don't know Eve," Zale insisted. "And I have no desire to save anyone but myself."

Once Clover was free, both he and Geth worked on Edgar. The beast seemed angry until Clover uncovered Edgar's eyes and let him see that the sycophant was there. Clover's presence calmed the Tangle immediately.

Anna untied Zale's right leg, and Zale jumped up to run off. Anna tackled Zale from behind. He flew to the ground, his face plowing into the dark dirt. Zale squirmed and fought, but he was so weak from years of doing nothing that Anna easily held him down.

Both Geth and Clover were impressed.

With Edgar freed, Geth bolted to Zale and took him out from under Anna. In the distance they could all see stalks of purple growth flying up into the air as something large thundered their way.

"Come with us," Geth urged. "We could use you."

"No," Anna replied.

Anna disappeared as Geth slung a kicking and screaming Zale over his shoulder. Clover swooped in behind the two of them, riding the head of Edgar. The Tangle grabbed Geth and Zale and took off running.

Payt was now less than a mile away.

Edgar ran through the fields of growth like a burrowing animal. Geth looked back and could see Payt getting closer, riding on top of a large wooden wagon as he had the night before.

Edgar sprinted as fast as he could, but the crops were troublesome to push through, and with the weight of Geth and Zale it wasn't easy for him to maintain their lead.

"They're getting closer!" Clover yelled.

Geth looked back. The wagon Payt drove was being pulled by a team of small horses. There were two other wagons behind him and hundreds of boors everywhere, running forward with their arms raised. The mass of inhumanity was tearing up the landscape as they thundered closer.

"Put me down!" Zale ordered.

Edgar broke from the field of tall purple stalks and out into a dusty stretch of weed-covered land. In the distance the unstable ground of Zendor was bubbling, sending large dirt pods up into the air.

Payt and the boors burst out from the field behind them, now only a few hundred feet away.

"Run through the unsteady ground," Geth hollered. "It'll make it harder on their wagons."

Edgar turned and ran straight toward the hundreds of dirt bubbles that were expanding and lifting up off the ground. Geth and Clover had previously ridden on one of the bubbles to make an escape. Unfortunately, the pods in this field weren't quite as large, and there wasn't time to climb onto one and have it expand beneath them without being caught.

"We can't go up," Clover yelled. "Those pods won't hold Edgar."

Edgar wove through the rising dirt wads, tiring with each step. The unstable ground made moving forward harder on the wagons, but it also made it almost impossible for Edgar to progress. Clover clung to the right horn on the Tangle's head and yelled into his ear.

"Keep going!"

Edgar picked up his speed as the boors closed in. Geth was still being held tightly with his brother. Their feet were dangling as Edgar ran.

"You should have left me!" Zale yelled. "We can't outrun that!"

Zale pointed back toward Payt. He and the boors were no more than two hundred yards away. Geth could see Payt's eyes fixed on him. The scratches Clover had dug across his face were red and thick. Payt smiled a wicked, no-room-for-mercy smile. Hundreds of boors ran in front of the wagon with their arms out and their slow minds fixed on nothing but getting to Geth and Zale.

Geth struggled in the arms of Edgar, trying to get out. "I need to stop Payt!"

"Really?" Clover asked incredulously. "Are you going to fight every single one of those boors in front of him?"

"If I need to," Geth answered loudly.

Dirt pods were rising and bursting all around them as Edgar struggled to keep his footing and move forward quickly. The temperamental ground rocked and gurgled.

"We're not going to—"

Clover never got a chance to finish his sentence. The soil directly in front of them crumbled and opened up. Dirt exploded as they dropped into a giant sinkhole and plummeted downward.

Payt pulled up on the reins, and his wagon spun and slammed to the ground, stopping just inches before the sinkhole. Hundreds of boors spilled like jacks into the opening behind Geth and the others. Payt held onto the overturned wagon, which saved him from falling into the hole and kept him safely on the ground.

Edgar roared as the massive dark hole swallowed its prey and belched up nothing but dirt.

## ✦ Chapter Six ✦

# DROP IT LIKE IT'S HOT

I like the dark. I have nothing against sunshine, but there's something comforting about a dark night. Many important discoveries have happened in the dark. Light, for one, would never have been invented had there not been a bit of black to illuminate. The game of hide-and-seek was created in the dark when a man had to feel his way around a room full of friends to find the light switch. And how fair would it really be if we were all able to "Guess who" without the darkness of someone's hands over our eyes? Dark serves a purpose. It enhances ghost stories, makes chocolate more mysterious, and gives flare guns a much better chance of being spotted. I like dark, but I'm not sure how to feel about the kind of dark that Geth and

Clover had been experiencing in Zendor. Not only were the nights starless and without a moon, but now, as they dropped from the bubbling field of dirt down hundreds of feet with dark boors falling behind them, they were having to deal with dark in a whole new light.

Clover screamed as he held tightly to the horns of Edgar. In a state of panic, Edgar had released Geth and Zale, and they were free-falling just above him.

"You have killed me!" Zale yelled as they plummeted.

"You're not dead yet," Geth hollered back.

Two seconds later their bodies splashed down into an underground lake filled with thick, warm water. They sank only a few feet as the gelatinous liquid absorbed most of the impact of their fall. Their bodies slapped up against the surface of the water, shocking and stinging their skin. Before they could even cry out, boors by the dozen dropped over and around them, splashing the thick water and creating massive ripples and waves.

They had fallen so far that there was no light visible from up above. The complete darkness caused the boors to freeze in the positions they had fallen in. Geth pushed two off of him as he tried to swim toward where he had heard Edgar hit.

"Clover!"

There was no answer.

"Clover!"

Edgar bellowed, and Geth could hear Zale complaining.

"I was content," Zale moaned. "I was safe. Look at me now. Wait, I can't see myself because we've fallen down a hole!"

"Calm down," Geth called out. "Do you have Clover?"

"No," Zale replied. "My beard's been ripped."

"That's not important," Geth said with bite. "Where's Clover?"

"Here!" Clover cried out from a fair distance away. "Over here!"

A small, dim light blinked on as Clover pulled out the last of the glow stones he had taken from the Stone Holders a few days ago. Geth looked toward the light and smiled.

"You okay?" Geth hollered.

"I'm fine," Clover yelled back. "A bunch of those boor guys fell on me. I think I'm stuck."

"Hold on," Geth replied.

Geth swam slowly through the gooey water. There were boors everywhere in the liquid and piled on top of each other. Geth's right ear smacked hard into one of the boors' heads. A crack echoed through the darkness. Geth shook it off and kept paddling toward the dim glow-stone light.

The heavy water was hard to swim in. It took ten good strokes before Geth could see the glow stone clearly. Clover was buried under three frozen boors. His hand was sticking out from under them with the glow stone in his palm. A couple of the boors in the water were blinking due to the weak light of the stone. The rest all stared blankly into the dark.

"Hurry," Clover said with an almost casual air from underneath the boors. "These guys don't smell good."

Geth swam up to the mass of bodies and pushed at the boors on top of Clover. Treading the thick liquid made it awkward and hard to get any real strength. The boors were twisted up together and wouldn't move. Geth tried to pull instead of push, but that was even less effective.

"Get them off of me," Clover insisted. "My forehead's wedged in this guy's armpit."

"There are too many on top of you," Geth said calmly. "I can't get any leverage in this water."

"Edgar!" Clover yelled, remembering there was something with considerably more strength nearby.

The sound of thrashing water and crashing boors

could be heard as Edgar frantically worked his way to Clover. The Tangle sank under a heavy pile of boors and then pushed back up to the surface. Edgar snorted and blew liquid all over. Geth wisely moved out of the way as Edgar threw his arms forward and blasted the boors from off of Clover. Clover rolled over on the body he had landed on and smiled up at Edgar. He spat something out of his mouth and held the glow stone over his head.

"Thanks," Clover said. "Apparently Geth can't tread and push at the same time."

Geth had already turned his attention from Clover to his brother.

"Zale!"

There was no answer. Clover hopped onto Edgar's head. He grabbed onto one horn with his left hand and held the glow stone up with the other. All three of them turned and began to swim back in the direction Geth had come from. Geth spotted Zale's head just bobbing above the water. Zale's eyes were open and staring straight forward. Geth treaded water next to his brother as Clover held the glow stone higher, trying to see any sign of dry land or an opening they could get out through.

"Can you see anything?" Geth asked.

"No," Clover said. "Well, I can see a bunch of those dirty boor guys. Wait."

"What is it?" Geth asked.

"I can see a dirty boor girl also."

"That doesn't change anything," Geth said.

"I just didn't want to be unfair," Clover explained. "Lilly's trying to get me to be more sensitive."

Geth and Edgar started to swim, but Zale just stayed there with his head bobbing in the thick water.

"Come on," Geth insisted.

Zale didn't say anything.

"Listen," Geth insisted, "you might not be right in the head right now, but I'm not leaving you here."

Zale stayed silent.

Geth wrapped his left arm around Zale's neck and began to swim, pulling him behind him. Zale didn't protest, but he didn't help, either. It was a struggle to paddle forward.

"Your brother's not as much fun as I thought he'd be," Clover observed from the top of Edgar.

"You thought he'd be fun?" Geth asked, breathing hard as he swam.

"I at least thought he'd be funner."

Edgar swam remarkably well for being such a massive creature with hooves for feet. He paddled with his large, thick arms and used his huge tail to propel him forward. There were oddly frozen boors all over the water's surface. It wasn't always easy or comfortable to move through them.

"We should be in Foo," Clover complained once more. "There are no boors in Foo. Well, except for that one guy who's always blathering on and on about his kids. He's a bore."

Geth stayed quiet.

"I mean, I'm all for adventure," Clover continued. "But this feels like it might end bad."

"Look," Geth said with excitement. "Is that a wall?"

Clover held the glow stone a little farther to the right, and they could clearly see the outline of a rock wall. Geth swam faster, pulling Zale behind. He got to the wall and reached out with his right hand to touch it. The stone wall was cold and as wet as the water. Geth kicked around with his feet trying to find a bottom or someplace to stand or climb onto—there was nothing.

"What now?" Clover asked.

"We'll follow the wall," Geth said, as if it were just a game. "It has to lead somewhere."

Geth and Edgar paddled along the side of the dark stone, searching for an opening or ledge. Clover moved onto Edgar's back, and the Tangle began to pound at the wall with his horns. A couple of stones broke loose above them and dropped into the water, barely missing

Clover. Edgar got hit on the head and bellowed accordingly. Zale took a stone to the left shoulder and bellowed vulgarly.

"Let's just keep following the wall," Geth instructed. "No more pounding."

"This could just be a big, round, underground lake," Clover pointed out. "There might not be a way out. We can't swim in circles forever."

"You're not swimming," Geth pointed out. "You're riding. I suppose we could just bob here until we perish."

"Fine," Clover said. "Keep swimming, Edgar."

Edgar and Geth continued to move along the wall, pushing boors out of the way and constantly kicking and grabbing for anything that looked solid. They reached a corner of the wall where the water ran down a five-foot-wide corridor. They headed down the passage without a thought.

Edgar barely fit in the small canal. His shoulders were inches from the sides. The ceiling of the passageway was eight feet up. It was covered in fuzzy moss that made their voices sound muted. The water was still too deep for them to feel a bottom anywhere.

The underground passage turned at a seventy-degree angle and then straightened out. Geth's legs and lungs burned from the constant paddling.

"You're insane," Zale said, putting in his negative two cents.

Geth stopped swimming and treaded water with his feet.

"You are heading into blackness," Zale complained. "The exit could be ten feet to your right and you'd never know it. More likely than not, there isn't an exit."

"I'm glad our father's no longer alive," Geth said seriously. "He would be disgusted with you."

"That's no concern of mine," Zale snipped.

Geth's blue eyes crackled under the weak light of the glow stone. He reached his hands up and pushed Zale all the way under the water. He held his brother down, making no motion to let him up.

"What are you doing?" Clover asked with interest.

"Reminding him that he wants to live," Geth said calmly, still holding Zale's head underwater.

Zale wasn't putting up any struggle.

"Most people remind each other with a phone call, or maybe those sticky little notes," Clover said, holding the glow stone out over the water directly above where Zale was being pushed down. "This looks more like murder than 'minder."

Edgar began to fidget, recognizing that something wasn't right.

"I have brothers," Clover tried to reason with Geth. "Sure, we've had our disagreements, but I've never threatened to drown them."

Zale was still being held underwater and making no effort to fight his way up and out of Geth's hold.

"Okay," Clover admitted, "I held one of my brothers under that one fountain. But that just got his hair wet. Besides, he had drawn on my face while I was sleeping."

There was still no struggle from Zale.

"Let him up," Clover suggested. "Please."

"He's a lithen," Geth said, as if he were answering a trivia question on a game show.

"He's going to be a dead lithen if you don't let go," Clover argued. "I know he's nuts, but you can't kill him."

Geth looked down at the water. The liquid was too dark to see beneath, but he could feel Zale down there.

"He's going to die," Clover begged.

Geth kept treading and holding Zale under.

"I'm telling Leven," Clover said. "I know I'm just a sycophant, but there—"

Zale burst up out of the water, gasping for breath and clawing at the air. He choked and coughed for a minute before finally calming down. Zale looked at his younger brother and spat. Geth just smiled.

"What are you trying to prove?" Zale asked.

"I knew you didn't want to die," Geth said. "Now come on."

Zale said a few choice things and then reluctantly began to swim after Geth.

"If we get out of here, I'm going to kill you," Zale insisted.

"Fine," Geth said.

"I'm serious," Zale complained. "I was safe and content in that prison cell, and you have made my life a dangerous bruise."

"At least you can describe it as a life now," Geth pointed out.

"I can remember a time when I believed that kind of rubbish," Zale spoke. "The lithen rhetoric is foolish and has no fit here."

"Hey," Clover said, trying to calm things down. "I don't even know what *rhetoric* means, but I don't think you need to be saying that."

"It doesn't matter," Geth debated. "He knows nothing of what he once believed."

"I know that fate dumped me here," Zale growled. "I've rotted for years without so much as a visit from fate."

"We're here now," Geth said.

"In a hole about to drown," Zale pointed out. "Fate should have sent an army. You and your rat will accomplish nothing but our deaths."

"Rat?" Clover asked, offended.

Zale didn't respond as all of them swam quietly down the waterway. Clover jumped off of Edgar and onto Geth's head. He leaned down and whispered in Geth's right ear.

"You should have held him under longer."

Geth nodded and continued to swim.

## ✦ Chapter Seven ✦

# WET BEHIND THE EARS

I have mixed feelings about mobs. On one hand, they're extremely good at holding torches, and they keep pitchfork salesmen in business. On the other hand, they seem a bit fanatical and touchy. Most mob scenes end with a street full of broken windows and people covered in pepper spray. I know from firsthand experience that angry mobs can make even the most confident of individuals feel bad about themselves. I remember how I felt while practicing my bassoon when large, angry mobs kept showing up at my doorstep and demanding that I stop. It's in moments like that when you begin to seriously doubt yourself.

People gathering can bring about mixed results.

Clover was a member of a two-man, one-sycophant,

one-Tangle mob. He was also seconds from crying when Geth's left foot finally knocked up against something solid. A couple of strokes later and the water they had been stuck in for so long was finally shallow enough for them to stand up in.

All of them crawled through the water until they reached a dry stretch of stone. Geth and Zale collapsed on the rock while Edgar shook the fur on his body and howled in relief. Clover set the glow stone down and tried to act like he was exhausted too.

"I'm going to be sore," Clover sighed.

"You are an impertinent creature," Zale said, coughing.

"Thanks," Clover replied, having no idea what impertinent meant.

After a few minutes of resting, Geth took the glow stone and stood up.

"I have no idea where we are," Geth admitted. "But unless we want to go back in the water, our only direction is forward."

"I'm done swimming," Zale growled.

"Forward it is," Geth said.

Geth began walking down the tunnel with Zale right behind him and Edgar and Clover taking up the rear. The tunnel got thinner and thinner as the ceiling and walls closed in. Edgar eventually had to walk hunched over to move through the passage. The ground they were walking on began to get sandy.

"The ground's changing," Geth observed.

"That's great," Zale said sarcastically. "Everyone rest easy, the ground's changing."

Geth spun around and hit his brother directly in the right ear. It wasn't the hardest hit, but it was enough to let Zale know that Geth was in no mood to be messed with. Geth was as surprised by what he had done as Zale was.

"Owww," Zale moaned, stopping to properly complain.

Edgar pulled up behind Zale, and Clover peered down from the top of Edgar's head.

"Wow," Clover said happily. "That is so un-Gethlike."

"I know," Geth agreed. "I'm not sure what's up with me. My insides are on fire."

"Actually, that could just be those Mips I gave you," Clover apologized. "The wrapper says they'll 'fill your gut and warm your cockles,' but I think they actually stuff your stomach and heat all your innards. I gave some to Leven last week and he threw up warm soup that he had never even eaten."

"It's not the Mips," Geth told Clover. "Although

thanks for the warning after the fact. I just wanted to hit Zale."

"This whole endeavor is futile," Zale complained. "You can hit me as much as you'd like, but there's no escaping Payt in this realm. He will find us. He will track us down, and the effects you feel from his voice at that moment will be nothing compared to what it will do to you in time. My mind is not my own. I know that, and I have come to terms with it. You, my little brother, are simply exhausting yourself before having to give up."

Geth hit Zale in the other ear.

"What was that for?" Zale complained.

"You said I could hit you as much as I'd like."

Geth turned from Zale and held the glow stone back out in front of him. He began to walk again. After two minutes Clover spoke.

"Are we there yet?"

"No," Geth replied. "But I think I can see light up ahead."

Geth began to run. Zale didn't pick up his speed, so Edgar pushed him forward in an effort to keep up with Geth. The light at the end of the tunnel grew exponentially. In a few moments it looked as if they were heading directly into the sun.

"Is that daylight?" Clover yelled.

"I don't think so," Geth yelled back.

The tunnel got even wider and the bright light lit up the high walls and ceilings. The source of the light was a large, round sphere sitting in a stone basin in the middle of a spacious cavern. The ball of light looked like a small star that had fallen from the sky and been swallowed by the earth. All around the light were other people. Some looked like cowboys and athletes; others were dressed as doctors and animal wranglers. All of them had black swaths of cloth tied over their eyes like blindfolds. A cowboy was walking around with a small wagon filled with glow stones while two men in business suits were stacking rocks near the bright star. The scene was remarkably quiet and as bright as any summer day.

Geth held his arm up over his eyes, unable to look directly at the light.

"A scorch stone," Zale said in awe.

"Who are the people?" Clover asked.

"Stone Holders," Geth whispered back. "I think they're making glow stones."

"So they're on our side," Clover said with relief.

"They're on *their* side," Zale said in a hushed voice. "They keep to themselves, hoping nothing will happen. It's a strategy I suggest everyone adopt. It has been rumored that they had the scorch stone, but it's never been seen by anyone I know of."

"Stay here," Geth instructed them.

Geth walked directly toward the scorch stone. He held his arm up over his eyes and looked down. The light was bright, but there seemed to be no heat coming off it. Geth looked to the side and saw three figures standing still and staring at the orb. He shuffled up to them and called out.

"Hello," Geth spoke loudly, his arm still in front of his eyes.

The three figures turned. It was hard to tell if they were looking right at Geth, due to the fact that their eyes were covered with black pieces of cloth. None of them responded.

"Are you Stone Holders?" Geth asked them.

"Yes," one of them replied.

"I'm—" Geth started to say.

"I know who you are," the same voice interrupted. "I was up in the caverns the other day when you were talking with Galbraith."

"Right," Geth said happily, acting as if they had just mentioned his best friend.

Galbraith wasn't Geth's best friend. Who he was was a Stone Holder that Clover and Geth had met a couple of days ago. He was a cowboy, and he had taken them to a big underground cave where he and a number of other Stone Holders had let Geth know that they had no desire to fight for what was right. It had been during that gathering that Clover had slipped off and stolen some food and the glow stones they had been using.

"Take this," one of the Stone Holders said, stepping up to Geth.

Geth could feel someone touch him on the right shoulder. He reached out. That same someone handed him a piece of cloth.

"Tie it around your eyes," the voice instructed.

Geth wrapped the piece of material around his eyes and tied it in the back. The material was thick and dark, but the light of the orb was so strong that Geth could see outlines and details of all those around him in a most remarkable way. It was as if his eyes were experiencing a completely new form of vision.

"Wow," Geth said. "I like this."

Geth could see the 3-D detail of the people near him. He saw that one of them was dressed as a boat captain and had a wooden leg. Another was a racecar driver, and a third looked like an astronaut. Apparently three children in Reality who had dreamed of the sea, the open road, and space now had their dreams stuck here in Zendor.

"How did you get here?" the astronaut asked.

"I fell in and swam," Geth replied. "Do you think you could lead us out of here?"

"I could," the boat captain said. "I may not have stars to guide me, but I can sail these caverns with ease."

"I'm just as capable," the astronaut spoke up, desperate to have a mission to perform.

"I'll drive him," the racecar driver insisted.

"You don't have a car," the boat captain reminded him.

"And you have no boat," the astronaut pointed out.

All three of them hung their heads in despair.

"I'm fine just walking," Geth insisted. "But we do need to get out of here."

"We?" the captain asked.

Geth pointed back behind him. Across the cavern, hidden at the entrance to the tunnel, Zale and Edgar were standing, both covering their eyes.

The astronaut swore.

"What is that thing?" the driver said.

"No need to worry," Geth assured them. "He's friendly."

"I don't understand," the astronaut said. "You

appear out of nowhere with a creature we've never seen. Did it come from down here?"

"No," Geth said. "Listen, will you take us out, or should we just try ourselves?"

The boat captain motioned for Geth to follow him and then turned and walked to the left. Geth retrieved his friends, and they followed the captain. The other Stone Holders in the cavern stopped what they were doing and turned their blindfolded eyes toward Edgar. Some mumbled and muttered, but most just stood still as the caravan of misfits walked through the space and into a tunnel at the opposite end of the cavern. The tunnel sloped upward and then became a set of wide stairs carved into the stone. The boat captain occasionally would mutter something sadly.

"Man the ballast."

The steps seemed to go on forever, and the sea captain's peg leg made an uncomfortable click against each stair. Clover was the first to complain, despite the fact that he was being carried by Edgar.

"Seriously," Clover said. "That clicking's the worst. And these stairs are so boring."

"Tell me again why people like sycophants?" Zale asked Geth, disgusted with Clover.

"I'll tell you," Clover volunteered.

Zale put his hands over his ears as Clover rambled.

" . . . We rarely use the word 'like' in a conversation. Also, most sycophants keep a good supply of tissue on hand. You never know when someone around you might need a little help beneath the nose. And we always . . ."

The stairs stopped at another cave where three other tunnels could be seen. The boat captain licked his finger, held it up, and then chose the right tunnel. Clover kept talking the entire time.

"Please," Zale begged, "I can't take it. Shut him up."

Clover looked around as if he didn't realize Zale was talking about him.

"Oh," Clover said, sulking. "I see how it is."

Clover whispered something into Edgar's right ear and disappeared.

After a few moments Edgar reached out and shoved Zale in the back of his right shoulder. Zale stumbled forward but kept walking. He gave Edgar a long, dirty look.

"Tell me again why people like sycophants?" Zale repeated.

"You should be happy," Geth said. "Clover's one of the best."

Zale shivered and kept walking.

## Chapter Eight

# BLINK TWICE IF YOU'RE SCARED

Sometimes I get confused. I know it's sort of demoralizing to hear that, but it's the truth. Not confused like, "Who am I," but confused like, "Where did I put that escape hatch, and why is there water filling up my underwater den?" Once I saw a woman buying an endangered whale with coins made from soap. The transaction wasn't all that confusing; I mean, who doesn't want a whale? What was confusing was the fact that I had never thought of using soap in such a way. My life would be crammed with gold-plated items if I had spent less time washing up and more time carving soap.

Well, Geth wasn't confused. The endless stairs

they were climbing eventually betrayed themselves and ended—in a big cave that looked almost identical to the cavern they had first been taken to days ago. There were long polished logs around the fire and furry rugs on the dirt floor.

"This is a main juncture," the boat captain said. "That tunnel there will lead you out." The captain pointed to a tunnel to their right. "It goes directly up above."

"Where's Galbraith?" Geth asked.

"Sleeping," the captain said. "That tunnel there leads to the sleeping quarters."

The captain took a moment to really look at Edgar. He shivered and continued. "If he were white, I'd go for my harpoon. Are you sure he's on our side?"

"No," Geth replied honestly. "But if I remember correctly, you guys really weren't on any side."

"That's true," the captain said. "It's safer that way."

"So sad," Geth replied, shaking his head.

"Probably," the captain agreed.

"Are there any here that would fight Payt?" Geth asked.

"Nope," the captain said, tapping his wooden leg against the ground. "We had an actual human snatched in from Reality a few months back. He was willing to fight."

"What happened?" Clover asked curiously.

"The boors caught him," the captain said. "The man built a wooden tower and moved it out onto the road. He put himself on the top and fired down at the boors with arrows. He thought he'd be safe, but the boors swooped in like a nor'easter, swarming in such large numbers that they picked up the entire tower and carried it, and the man, to Pencilbottom Castle. Payt seduced him with his voice, and now that same man fights as a boor against us."

"No," Clover said, bothered. "Not what happened to *him*—what happened to your leg?"

The captain looked down at his peg leg. "I know nothing of my life before Zendor," he told Clover. "Some of us make up backstories for our lives, but not me."

"Seriously," Clover whispered to Geth, "what kid in Reality is dreaming of being a captain with a peg leg?"

The sound of a commotion could be heard down the stairs they had just climbed. At first the noise was faint, but, like a scream building strength, it intensified until it burst from behind them like a frightening hiss.

"Something wicked this way blows!" the captain bellowed.

Cowboys and athletes and Stone Holders of all shapes and occupations burst out from the tunnels below.

"Run!" someone screamed. "Run!"

Geth didn't move, but Zale took off for the exit with Edgar and Clover following.

"What's happening?" Geth asked, wanting to charge back down the stairs and beat something up.

"Gas!" a businessman yelled, waving his briefcase as he ran. "Smoke!"

Geth saw the racecar driver he had talked to earlier. He grabbed him and held him back.

"What's going on?"

"There's some sort of fog," he panicked. "It's thick around turn three and coming from the direction you appeared. People breathing it were falling to the ground. I think they're dead. Now let me go, it's still coming!"

Galbraith the cowboy emerged from the tunnel that led to the sleeping quarters. Geth let go of the driver and called after Galbraith. The cave was too loud for him to hear, and Galbraith was running too fast to be caught.

More Stone Holders ran past Geth and out toward the exit tunnel. A scientist fell to the ground and was being trampled by his fellow Stone Holders. Geth

75

pushed people away from him and helped him up. The man adjusted his glasses.

"My hypothesis is flawed," he yelled before running away.

Since Geth had no way of actually beating up gas, he decided to sprint with the crowd toward the exit. For a bunch of grown men, everyone around him sounded a lot like a crowd of screaming little girls.

The tunnel leading out was short, and at the end there was a large section of ivy and moss that hid the entrance. As Geth emerged, he could see hundreds of Stone Holders, who were unaccustomed to being in the light, standing there with their hands over their eyes, blinking under the sun and trying to breathe in clean air.

Clover appeared on Geth's shoulder.

"Where's Zale?" Geth yelled.

"With Edgar at the edge of the field," Clover replied. "What's happening?"

"There's some sort of gas coming up from the bottom of the caves," Geth said. "My guess is that Payt threw something down the hole we fell into. He's smoking us out."

Stone Holders continued to flow out of the opening and into the daylight. All of them were crippled by the strong sun they rarely saw. Their eyes fluttered and blinked as they tried to see anything besides a glowing dot. Geth looked around in concern.

"This isn't right," he said. "Look how vulnerable they are."

"Does that mean unattractive?" Clover asked. "If so, I agree—everyone's so dirty here."

"No, it means if Payt were to—"

Geth wasn't able to finish because boors by the hundreds emerged from a break in the fields and stormed in on the impromptu gathering of stunned Stone Holders. For being such a dumb and thoughtless group of individuals, the boors were remarkably good at attacking. The dark, barky boors wrapped their arms and legs around the Stone Holders and bound them like rope. For every boor that bound someone up, two more boors would arrive. Almost instantly the Stone Holders were outnumbered and being completely wrapped up.

Geth could see Zale voluntarily trying to give himself up to an approaching boor. Geth dashed in and with a swift kick crushed the knees of the boor and sent him crumbling backward. Edgar began swinging his long arms and bowling over dozens of boors with each twist of his upper body.

Clover, keeping invisible, leapt from boor to boor, slashing at their arms and legs. Geth saw three go down as Clover swiped his claws at the back of all three of their legs.

Geth grabbed Zale.

"Let me go!" Zale demanded. "Let me give up."

Zale hit Geth in the chest, but with his arms being so weak and unused, the hit barely registered. Clover witnessed the incredibly feeble blow.

"Maybe we don't really want him," Clover said, embarrassed for Zale.

Geth fought off a boor with one arm and held onto Zale with the other as more and more barky beings filled the landscape and locked down every last Stone Holder.

"We have to run!" Clover said.

"No way," Geth insisted, punching a tall, dark boor in the ribs.

"There's too many!" Clover yelled.

Boors were filling up every inch of space. Edgar was no longer on the offense but on the defense, simply trying to keep the boors from overcoming him. Clover jumped from Geth and onto Edgar. He yelled something in the Tangle's ear. The beast swung around in a complete circle, sending boors flying in all directions. He then lunged and caught Geth off guard.

Edgar wrapped his arms around Geth and Zale and held them both so tightly that their faces became red. He twisted, and with huge, high leaps he bounded across the ground and into the trees where so many of the boors had just come from. Edgar crashed through branches and bushes and out into a cluster of tall rocks. The stones jutted up out of the soil like rockets that had been frozen at blastoff. Edgar moved behind the rocks and pushed his back up against a cracked slab as if to hide. No boors had followed, but they could hear the commotion of the captured Stone Holders on the other side of the boulders. Edgar turned and stepped to one side just enough so that they could all see out though a break in the rocks.

Edgar was holding both Geth and Zale in front of him with Clover on his head. From their vantage point they could all see the last few Stone Holders being wrapped up by boors. Zale tried to yell out and get captured, but Edgar brought his tail around and with the tip of it covered Zale's mouth. Geth was struggling to get out as well, but his wish was to single-handedly take on the hundreds of boors that were now there.

"Let me go," Geth whispered harshly.

"You know how much I hate being the voice of reason," Clover argued. "But you can't beat them."

Geth was going to argue some more, but the sound of something happening on the other side of the rocks stole his attention. Through the crack they could see the boors shifting and moving as something else came into view. They heard the horses and knew Payt was arriving.

As the horse's hooves clicked, they could all see the wagon coming into view, with Payt sitting on the front of it and Eve by his side. Eve's expression was as blank as the sky. Under the influence of Payt's voice, she was nothing but a shell. Next to Eve were a couple of Payt's lead boors. Payt himself appeared angry, and the claw marks across his face made him look considerably more frightening than he once had.

Geth's heart ricocheted wildly against his ribs. It was one thing for Clover to stop him from picking on the boors, but it was another thing entirely to deny him the right to pick on Payt.

"Let me go," Geth insisted.

"Shh," Clover said soothingly.

Edgar trembled uneasily at the sight of Payt.

Payt climbed down from the wagon and onto the ground. He looked at all the Stone Holders as his boors held them tightly.

"Well, well," Payt said with arrogance to the crowd. "Who knew that a dirty lithen would help me finally discover where some of the Stone Holders have been hiding? Perhaps there's value in a lithen after all."

Payt looked closely at a couple of the Stone

Holders. His boors held onto their victims, making no noise. A few of the Stone Holders squirmed and muttered, but most of them stood captive in a silence of resignation and defeat.

"Now," Payt hollered out at the crowd, "who has Geth?"

When nobody replied, Payt continued.

"Did he die when he fell down that hole?"

Nobody answered.

Galbraith was being held by two thick boors. One was wrapped around him like a sleeping bag and the other one was holding him at the shoulders. Payt stepped up to Galbraith and smiled.

"Do you know who I am?" Payt asked.

Galbraith just stared forward.

"Do you know what happened to those lithens?" Payt tried. "I chased them down the same hole I used to smoke you out."

Galbraith didn't look up.

"Let's hope for the sake of Zendor that they're dead," Payt hollered. "Of course, for your sake it won't make a difference."

Payt leaned in closer to Galbraith and whispered in his right ear. Every captive Stone Holder lifted his head to see what Payt was doing. Galbraith's eyes widened as if in shock. His eyelids then closed and reopened slowly. Payt's voice had begun to conquer another mind.

"What an easy recruit you'd be," Payt said, sounding bored. "But you're not worth my breath. Release him."

The two boors holding onto Galbraith let go of him. The Stone Holder remained standing there and looking forward.

Payt lifted his right leg and kicked Galbraith as hard as he could in the chest. The defenseless Stone Holder flew backward and hit the ground violently.

"Pathetic," Payt said. "You wouldn't have lasted a day in Reality."

Payt walked back to the wagon and addressed the large boor that was holding the reins of the horses.

"You," Payt said coolly. "I want you to stay here."

The big boor climbed off the wagon.

"I could talk at all of these fools and bring them over to my side," Payt said sternly to the large boor. "Heaven knows their brains are pathetic enough. But I think I'll use this moment to teach Zendor a lesson. I want you to destroy them all," Payt ordered.

The Stone Holders who were held captive and had been silent up until now began to plead and beg for mercy from Payt.

"You want mercy?" Payt yelled angrily. "You're talking

to the wrong person. I didn't become a fourteenth-level medieval warrior in the nonfairy division by possessing mercy. I know how to rule. Now, kill them all."

Geth pushed at Edgar, trying to get out, but the huge Tangle kept a tight hold. Through the crack in the rocks they could see Payt ride off in the wagon with Eve by his side.

"They won't really kill them, right?" Clover whispered.

The moment the wagon was out of view, the large boor that Payt had left in charge made a gesture to the others with his arms. The other boors began to tighten their arms and steal the lives of the Stone Holders they were wrapped around. Zale watched in horror as Clover cried and looked away. Geth screamed and hollered, but the sounds of Stone Holders doing the same thing and with much more volume drowned out his anguish.

Clover couldn't take the awful scene any longer. He leaned down and in a whimper instructed Edgar to go. Edgar shifted to face the east and began to run.

◆ Chapter Nine ◆

# PULLED APART AND TORN ASUNDER

In a national survey that I just made up, sadness was ranked as the number-one cause of sorrow. Now, perhaps I'm being too technical, but being bummed out can cause major discomfort. It can lead to things like anguish and even full-on lamentation. Of course, I don't mention this to make you upset, I mention this to let you know that life is best enjoyed when you steer clear of unnecessary situations that may cause unhappiness. Stay away from crumbling buildings with poor foundations. Don't hang out in a shark tank dressed as meat. And please, if it's at all possible, never let a person like Payt have even a little bit of power. Almost always it will lead to an overall feeling of misery, despair, hopelessness, and defeat. Sorry to go all thesaurus on you, but no matter how you say it, sadness stinks.

Edgar ran as fast as he could while holding Geth and Zale tightly. Sadness chased them like a wolf nipping at their heels. The Tangle was a simple, frightening beast, but even he understood how important it was to get as far away as possible from what was happening.

Geth, on the other hand, felt they were heading in the wrong direction. He kicked his heels into Edgar and threw his head back, trying to crack him in the chest. When neither of those things worked, Geth leaned forward and bit Edgar's arm as hard as he could.

The Tangle roared from the shock of the bite.

Edgar opened his arms, and Geth and Zale dropped out. Zale sputtered and rolled into a ditch while Geth used the momentum of his fall to spring back up and begin running toward the spot they had just come from, leaving Edgar and Zale behind. Clover leapt onto Geth's shoulder as he ran.

"You can't do this," Clover said, using his best dad voice. "There are too many."

"Too many for what?" Geth yelled. "They're dying."

"We'll probably die too," Clover informed him.

"There are worse fates," Geth insisted. "And I'll sleep easier dead than if I don't try."

"Do people sleep when they're dead?" Clover yelled.

Geth was too busy running to respond.

Geth hurdled over a short wall of stone and ran directly into the gathering of boors. They were all still slowly squeezing the breath from the captured Stone Holders. Like snakes choking the life out of a victim they constricted. Some of the Stone Holders were red in the face or near passing out. Geth grabbed the nearest boor and ripped him off of the Stone Holder he was squeezing. He hit the boor in the jaw and kicked out his legs. With the boor on the ground, Geth administered a single hit to the face, and the poor mindless boor was out.

Geth ran to Galbraith, who was still lying on the ground in a daze from Payt's kick. Geth pulled him up and tried to shake some sense into him.

"Come on!" Geth yelled at Galbraith. "Get up and fight."

Galbraith just stood there as Geth knocked out a second boor and Clover began slashing up a third. Two more Stone Holders were freed, but still none of them were moving.

"Galbraith!" Geth barked. "They're going to die."

Geth reeled back and gave Galbraith a sharp hit on the right ear. The blow seemed to wake Galbraith up.

"Fight!" Geth ordered.

Geth turned and beat at the boor behind him. The boors lacked the ability to think for themselves. They knew only what they had been told to do. The second they were pulled off of their victims, their singular focus was on reattaching themselves and continuing to strangle. It made it easy for Geth and the others to simply pull them off and knock them out as they struggled to get back to strangling.

"There's so many!" Galbraith yelled as he looked around and witnessed all the Stone Holders that were slowly being choked to death.

"Then go faster!" Geth ordered, unmoved by the impossibility of it all.

Clover sliced up the back of a barky boor and quickly leapt to another, where he cut off a good chunk of her dirty hair. Each boor he messed with would momentarily release its grip, giving the Stone Holder it was suffocating a chance to breathe.

"Keep doing that!" Geth cheered. "It'll buy us some time."

As each boor was pulled off and knocked out, a new Stone Holder would join the fight. Some Stone

Holders took a few moments to commit to doing battle, but once they saw that it was making a difference, they got at it.

Exhausted, Clover leapt to another and jammed his claws into the boor's arms. The boor screamed and released its victim while another Stone Holder swooped in and knocked the boor out.

Geth could barely lift his arms any longer as he looked out at the hundreds of Stone Holders still being squeezed to death. His forces were growing in number, but so many were exhausted, and some Stone Holders were seconds away from dying by strangulation.

Geth heard a thundering noise from behind him. He turned to defend himself and saw Edgar charging toward the group. Edgar instantly began to pound and knock out any boor still standing.

Clover smiled proudly.

Edgar was a welcome sight, but they still needed more help. As if on cue, Anna sprang from a field to the left with her troops following behind her.

Geth smiled wide.

"I can see that," Clover chastised. "You didn't smile when Edgar arrived."

Hundreds of women emerged from the fields and began to fight alongside the Stone Holders. For the first time in the battle, the numbers favored Geth's group. The women beat at the backs of the boors with sticks while Stone Holders pulled them down and knocked them out. A couple of girls dressed as cheerleaders flew through the air and administered kicks to the faces of boors. A woman dressed in a karate outfit took down a fat boor that was choking the life out of a thin Stone Holder.

"Happy to see us?" Anna hollered as she fought alongside Geth.

"Very," Geth hollered back.

"Payt's burning our fields," Anna yelled, beating the back of a boor so that it would release a cowboy Stone Holder. "It might be time for us to consider fighting back."

The boor let go of the Stone Holder and passed out against the ground.

Anna twirled and then leaped her way over to free another. Stone Holders and the women of Those Who Hide fought beautifully for being a group of people that had just stood by and watched for so long.

A few minutes later the fight was over. Six Stone Holders had been strangled, but the majority had been saved. All the boors were bound with ropes of witt and pinned to the ground by Anna and her girls.

Galbraith lay on the ground like a hyperventilating corpse trying to catch his breath and come to terms with the fact that he had actively fought against Payt. Geth and Clover and Edgar gathered around him and sat down.

"You okay?" Geth asked.

"I reckon so," Galbraith said, reminding Geth that he was a cowboy in every sense of the word. "That's a funny-looking horse you have."

Edgar snorted, and Clover patted him behind the ears.

"Payt was going to kill us all," Galbraith continued. "He almost did. In the past, he would capture, but now he brings death."

The sound of rustling in the field behind him caused Geth to turn and stop talking. Geth looked up to see a somber-looking Zale walking back from where he had so valiantly hidden.

"Thanks for helping," Clover said sarcastically.

"I was hiding and thinking," Zale said weakly.

Edgar snorted.

"I'd say I'm sorry," Zale snipped, "but I'm still alive. And I know what we must do."

"We?" Geth asked happily.

"We should find Lars," Zale said. "That woman is right. He is the key to surviving Payt."

"Lars," Galbraith said almost reverently.

"I'm glad the lithen thinks I'm right," Anna said,

walking up to the group. "Lars is quite wise; he's helped countless beings in need."

"And there are other Stone Holders near Lars," Galbraith said with excitement. "If we were to meet with them, we would have quite a force."

"Does that mean you'll fight?" Geth asked.

"I was sleeping," Galbraith said softly. "I was sleeping and when I woke up I was almost strangled to death and then I was kicked to the ground like a dog. I figure if I'm not safe sleeping, I probably need to do something to fix it."

"What about you, Anna?" Geth asked.

"We don't want to be involved," she said. "But we can see now that we have no choice. Payt's burning our fields, killing anyone who stands in his way. It looks like the return of the lithens has brought us a lot of danger. Some of us wonder if you and your brother aren't the problem."

"Do you?" Geth asked.

"No," Anna replied. "I know that Payt is the cause of our misery, but I still fear the fight."

"Great," Clover moaned. "There's no way Geth doesn't follow that with some inspirational saying."

Geth stared at Clover.

"Really?" Clover asked. "You weren't thinking of something to say? How about, 'The only fight to fear is the fear we fight'? or maybe, 'Fear is the one thing that fighting takes tips from'?"

"That's confusing," Anna said coldly to Geth. "Were you really going to say that?"

"Not exactly," Geth joked.

"It would have been close," Clover said.

"So what's the next move?" Anna said. "This victory is only going to make Payt angrier."

"We find this Lars," Geth said. "I can see no harm in seeking out someone wiser."

"He is a rare voice of wisdom in this realm," Anna said, stretching her hands into fifth position and acting like the ballerina she was.

"It's about a two-day hike across Zendor," Galbraith said. "The Stone Holders in that area know his whereabouts."

"Will he fight with us?" Geth asked.

"It's doubtful," Galbraith said. "His passion is peace."

"I have the same passion," Geth admitted. "But sometimes peace needs a push."

"His support would go far," Anna said honestly.

"Then let's move," Geth said, excited to not only have a plan but also volunteers that were finally willing to fight. "We can gather others as we move."

"There are women in the field around the

mountains where Lars lives," Anna added. "I know them well."

"Good," Geth said. "We'll move immediately. We'll travel through the fields as far as we can and then wait until night to go farther."

"What about our caves here?" Galbraith asked. "We have a load of supplies down there, not to mention the scorch stone."

"Leave it for now," Geth said. "It's not safe if there's still gas in there. But trust me, one day soon you will be able to come and go anywhere in Zendor as freely as you please. Payt will not prevail."

Anna and Galbraith looked at each other. Galbraith smiled and "yee-hawed." Even Zale got into the action by looking at least two shades happier than miserable.

"We're willing to follow," Anna reiterated. "But we still have our doubts of succeeding."

"That's enough for now," Geth said thankfully.

Anna gathered her troops, which consisted of just over a hundred women. The Stone Holders had twice as many. With everyone organized, they set off walking side by side in a tight line.

The war was on.

## ◆ Chapter Ten ◆

# SMELL OF SMOKE

Y ou don't want to make me angry. Not that I'll go all nuts on you, but as a human you just really shouldn't want to make another human angry. I don't want to make you mad. In fact I'd prefer to make you happy or contented—or amazed by how I tell the story of Foo. Of course, if you are amazed, it's most likely because Foo and all its inhabitants are awe worthy. Take Geth, for example. As a child, Geth rarely knew anger—actually, as an adult, Geth rarely knew anger. In fact, it was only with the addition of Ezra that Geth began to feel and experience true frustration. Now, with the effect of Payt's voice on Geth's soul, not only was he able to feel anger, but he was fantastic at displaying it. It wasn't the kind of anger you might see from another driver after you cut him off. And it certainly wasn't the same kind of anger I experienced after poisoning the wrong criminal. No, the anger Geth displayed was a complete hatred of all things evil or wrong. His desire to move fate in an aggressive and powerful direction bled into every cell he had. There's no reason to fear Geth's anger—unless, of course, you are an enemy of fate. In which case it's probably best to just hide and hope things blow over.

Geth and Clover sat by the small stream at the edge of the field and waited impatiently for the sun to go down. Edgar was asleep, hidden in the field and snoring loud enough to give the stream a little competition in the sound-effects department. Their group had traveled far through the day, but now they were forced to wait until dark to move safely across a large, empty stretch of Zendor and into the mountains on the far side. There had been no sign of Payt, although the air smelled faintly of smoke from the fires with which he had been terrorizing other parts of Zendor. The day had been long and smoky.

Earlier in their travels, a number of the women had insisted on walking right next to Geth. Clover in turn had been constantly reminding Geth that Phoebe was in Foo at the moment being faithful to him.

"Again," Geth insisted as he and Clover finally sat alone. "My heart belongs to Phoebe."

"Right," Clover said. "I just think it speaks volumes about your relationship that she doesn't even know where you are right now."

"Does Lilly know where you are?" Geth asked.

"Sycophants are different," Clover said, waving. "She knows I'm alive."

"But missing," Geth reminded Clover.

"Sure, but in fairness to Lilly, I'm missing a lot," Clover said. "Remember that week I got trapped in that hole?"

"Yeah," Geth laughed. "You could have just let go of that stick and you would have been able to fit out."

"It was a great stick," Clover said defensively. "I didn't want anyone else to come and take it. Besides, this isn't about me. I'm just saying, it might be a nice gesture if you called Anna *Phoebe* instead. You know, to help keep Phoebe on your mind."

"I think that would be insulting to Anna," Geth pointed out.

"See," Clover argued. "You take her side a lot. I'm going to be honest, that looks suspicious."

"What did I ever talk about before I knew you?" Geth mused affectionately.

"The fact that you can't remember shows pretty clearly that it probably wasn't important," Clover said.

Zale came over and took a seat next to Geth. Zale's dark eyes seemed clearer and more attentive than before. He had also taken a swim in the stream so he was cleaner and looked considerably less like a vagrant.

"It feels so odd," Zale said. "Not being locked up. Looking at the sky and knowing that I won't sleep in a cell tonight."

"Think how it will feel once all of Zendor can stand freely in the open."

"I suppose," Zale said. "It's just easier for me to feel good about things if I know they will benefit me personally."

"Wow," Geth said with disgust. "You're far from impressive."

"And you're on a fool's errand," Zale said candidly. "I know what Payt is capable of. He has no sympathy or mercy, and an almost endless supply of boors stands at his service. He will be impossible to defeat."

"Noooo," Clover said, digging at his own forehead. "Don't get Geth started with that impossible stuff."

Geth kept quiet and reached out to scratch Clover behind the ears.

"You know nothing of hope," Zale said with

sincerity. "Darkness ascends and hope is but a pill that prolongs the suffering."

"Darkness doesn't ascend," Clover complained. "It settles."

"You'll feel differently once we finish this and return to Foo," Geth told Zale, trying to keep his insides from becoming worked up over the stupid things his brother was saying. "Besides, I find hope in the darkest days, and focus in Foo."

"I don't even remember Foo," Zale continued. "I can recall bits and pieces, but my mind is not my own. I do remember our parents. I know they were kind."

"They were," Geth agreed. "And they'd be disgusted with you."

"I don't care one way or the other," Zale said. "Fate was their way. Nothing surprised them or concerned them. They felt no disappointment."

"They knew sorrow," Geth said. "But they knew that bitterness never lasts. Even the strongest flavors fade."

Clover cringed.

"Why are you making that face?" Zale asked Clover. "Is that directed at me?"

"No," Clover said, rolling his eyes at Zale. "Not everything's about you. For your information, I was making that face because of what Geth said.

Sometimes your brother gets a little wordy. 'Even the strongest flavors fade.'"

"It's true," Geth pointed out.

"Maybe," Clover replied. "But if I were your biographer I'd never include that line."

"My biographer?" Geth asked.

"Yeah," Clover said, looking at both lithens. "What? Don't you ever pretend that a biographer is following you around taking notes?"

"No," Geth said.

"That's weird," Clover said, shrugging. "Well, if I was your biographer I wouldn't write down some of the things you say. Or maybe I'd write them down, but I'd change them a bit. I'd also make you have a mustache."

"I do remember sycophants," Zale said, looking intently at Clover. "But I don't remember them ever speaking their minds so freely."

"Clover is an exception to almost every rule," Geth informed him.

"Well, don't you wish he would just hold his tongue on occasion?" Zale asked honestly.

Clover put his hands on his hips and tried to look offended. Geth patted the sycophant on the head.

"Not at all," Geth replied. "I'd rather hear him

speak than listen to some of the garbage you're spewing."

Zale looked at Geth and then turned to Clover. "You're right; he does get a little wordy."

"I can't tell if I should feel happy or sad about being right," Clover said, confused.

The sky began to dim as darkness finally began to work its way onto the landscape and settle over them.

Anna and a woman in a lab coat approached Geth. Anna wanted to know when they would be leaving and the woman in the lab coat wanted to know if Geth thought she was pretty.

"In about ten minutes," Geth answered. "And as beautiful as my sister."

The woman in the lab coat looked crestfallen. Apparently she didn't want to be Geth's sister. She sulked off while Anna stayed. Anna stared at Geth and then Zale. She tilted her head and blinked.

"I'll be honest," Anna said respectfully. "When Eve used to talk about the return of the lithens, I didn't think it would look like this."

Geth and Zale looked at each other.

"You are here, I can see that," Anna said sincerely. "But we won't succeed."

"I've been trying to tell him that," Zale pointed out.

"Why don't you two just get married," Clover said, bothered. "Then you can both spend your days talking about how nothing will work."

"See," Zale complained to Geth. "He really should hold his tongue."

Clover disappeared as the night deepened. It was now Galbraith's turn to walk up and join the conversation.

"We're ready when you are," Galbraith said, still trying to feel comfortable in the role of someone who was committed to the cause. "Actually, we're not that ready, but we will follow you."

Geth stood up. "Wake any who have been sleeping and make sure they all have their stones."

The sun completely disappeared and black dripped around them like burnt molasses.

"See?" Clover argued. "That is not ascending."

Clover reached into his void and pulled out his glow stone. Galbraith retrieved one from his pocket, and Anna pulled hers from a pouch on the side of her leg.

In the glow of the stones Geth nodded at Galbraith. Galbraith stuck two of his fingers in his mouth and whistled shrilly. All throughout the fields of witt and crops, hundreds of glow stones blinked on.

The sight of all those who were now willing to sort of fight for Zendor made Geth's heart sort of glad.

"I bet this makes you happy," Clover said quietly from Geth's left shoulder. "I mean, all these people willing to rough up Payt."

"It makes me happy to know that it won't just be you and me," Geth said back.

"Of course, we *could* take him ourselves," Clover bragged.

"Of course," Geth agreed.

"It's pretty gracious of us to share the fight," Clover said.

"Extremely," Geth replied.

Clover hopped off of Geth and went to wake up Edgar. The Tangle woke easily and joined the band of glowing stones and nervous hearts. They had a long night of walking ahead of them.

## Chapter Eleven

# CAUGHT OFF GUARD

I don't trust numbers. To me math has always been sneaky and something to be cautiously suspicious of. Two plus two equals four? Who really knows for sure? When I received two mysterious gifts in the mail they caused five very real problems. Where's the logic in that? And how do you explain the fact that when I left the train station transporting six spies who had committed twelve international violations, traveling eighty miles an hour for two days, I ended up with one very severe headache and the remainder of a once-complete map?

It just doesn't add up.

To get to the far corner of Zendor, it was necessary to leave the main road and cut diagonally across the landscape. As the hundreds of Stone Holders and women marched through the dark night, the glowing stones in their palms made them look like a parade of fireflies. The land they were crossing now was dusty and dry. It was also unsteady and constantly gurgling and groaning, making the dark hike even more uneasy.

Geth led the procession, with Galbraith and Anna a few paces behind. Clover was riding on Geth's head due to the fact that Edgar smelled sort of funny and was really jarring when he walked. Edgar was near the middle of the pack, directly behind Zale.

"This part's kinda boring," Clover sighed atop Geth's head.

"Sorry," Geth joked. "Maybe we'll get attacked or fall into some new hole soon."

"Promise?" Clover replied, only half joking. "My arm's getting tired from holding this glow stone."

"I'll make sure to tell Lilly about that," Geth said.

"Actually," Clover corrected, "I could hold this stone all night."

"All right," Geth replied. "I'll tell Lilly that instead."

Clover sighed.

"Are you going to be okay?" Geth asked, half serious.

"Probably not," Clover admitted. "And I wanna

go on record as saying that we should have never come here."

"We didn't come here," Geth reminded Clover. "We were captured."

"And now we're fighting to get back to Foo?" Clover asked hopefully.

"What we're doing is the right thing," Geth said kindly. "Where we end up because of it shouldn't be our concern."

"Maybe it's just the fact that you and I have been spending a lot of time together lately," Clover observed. "Or maybe it's because I'm tired. Either way, the things you are saying are kinda making me feel sick."

"It's probably because you're tired," Geth said.

"Right," Clover agreed.

The dry, sandy ground they were walking on became partly rocky. Soon the sand was a thing of the past and all they could see beneath them was stone. Galbraith caught up to Geth.

"We Stone Holders are getting tired," he said. "Maybe we could rest?"

"We'll find a place before the light," Geth said. "We have at least three more hours of black and I want to get as far as we can under the cover of this night."

"To be honest with you," Galbraith began, "this is more work than we were prepared for."

Geth didn't know if he should laugh or chastise.

"We would have been safe underground," Galbraith continued. "Had you and your menagerie of animals not fallen in on us, we'd be protected and rested in our caves."

"This is not the time to lose the vision," Geth said with authority. "We're doing this for you. Have you already forgotten what almost happened when you were last sleeping?"

"Sorta," Galbraith said. "A number of us are talking about how this should just be your fight."

It was dark, but even in the soft light of the glowing stones one could see the flush of red growing up Geth's neck.

"I can't make you want this," Geth said, completely bothered by the shifting commitment. "If you bow out, then we'll carry on without you."

"That seems like a good solution," Galbraith said. "You can do it. Actually . . . we don't believe that you can."

Geth stopped and spun around to look Galbraith directly in the eyes. The line of followers behind them came to a sudden halt as hundreds of them bumped into one another.

"Listen," Geth said strongly, "you're a dream. You didn't even exist before you were dreamt into Zendor, but now you do. I've seen you have fear and even hope. I know you want more and you probably don't know how to go about getting it. Well, I'm going to show you. I'm going to make it clear that the life you now live is nothing but the opening to a real existence."

Galbraith just stared at Geth.

"Maybe you should use more cowboy words," Clover suggested.

"You know what I mean, don't you?" Geth asked Galbraith.

"We don't know how to be anything but useless," Galbraith said honestly. "We have farmed and kept alive, but this is not what we know."

"Do you know how to walk?" Geth asked.

"Of course," Galbraith said. "I've been doing that since I got here."

"Perfect," Geth said. "All I need from you is to keep walking."

Galbraith stared at Geth's blue eyes. After a few moments of heavy silence, he spoke.

"We can walk," he said.

Geth turned around and began moving forward again. It took a few moments, but Galbraith and all the entire procession finally followed after him.

"Eventually they're going to have to do more than walk," Clover whispered to Geth.

"I know," Geth whispered back. "Hopefully by then I'll have tricked them into fighting."

"You lithens are a sneaky bunch," Clover said. "You're like those aggressive lady men in Reality."

"Lady men?" Geth asked, confused.

"You know, the ones with the big noses and shoes."

"You mean clowns?" Geth asked.

Clover shivered and disappeared.

The procession continued to move at a good clip. The rocky ground around them began to rise up, and soon they were walking through a canyon with polished granite walls that were higher than the glow stones could light up. Geth slowed down a bit so that Galbraith could catch up.

"Where are we?" Geth asked the cowboy.

"This here's the granite passage," Galbraith answered. "Say something loud."

"Lilly!" Clover yelled while invisible and still on Geth's head.

*Lilly, Lilly, Lilly.*

The echo was clear and almost soothing in the silent night.

"The slick stone makes remarkable noises,"

Galbraith said. "Beyond this is the Orange River, and past that are the fields and mountains that hide the other women. Lars lives beyond the mountains."

Anna came running up from the middle of the line. She touched Geth on the right elbow and he turned to look at her. Her expression was as messy as the hair that hung in front of her face.

"We don't like this," Anna said as a matter of fact.

"Like what?" Geth asked, continuing to walk through the granite passage.

"This territory," Anna said. "We don't know where we are, and there's nowhere to hide in this canyon."

"We're all hidden," Geth reminded her. "The dark has us disguised, and we'll be out of this passage and into the fields before light arrives."

"It's not right," Anna insisted. "It feels wrong."

"I think it feels dark and long," Clover said. "I'm not sure why Geth and I are—"

"Stop."

"Fine," Clover said hurt. "I'll keep my feelings—"

"Stop."

The word was strong and resonated through everyone like a deep plunk of bass.

"Stop now."

Everyone stopped walking. They all looked around, wondering where the voice was coming from.

Clover hopped up onto Edgar. The Tangle wrapped the tip of his tail around Zale's right wrist and began to chase after Geth, pulling Zale behind him. Zale was forced to keep running or fall and be dragged.

"Let me go!" Zale screamed.

Edgar roared in such a way that Zale understood the need to stop complaining.

By the time the first light of day began to appear they had crossed the Orange River and reached the far corner of Zendor. The fields here were filled with ten-foot-high stalks of gray corn and purple witt that hid them easily in the light. They moved down the rows looking for a spot to rest. Geth kept his eyes peeled for any sign of boors from behind as well as any women in the field they were now in.

"I know there are women around us," Geth said.

"Seriously," Clover chastised. "You're not in this for the girls, remember."

"I mean Those Who Hide," Geth clarified. "Anna said there were a number of her type in this area."

"You think they're hiding in this stuff?" Clover asked.

"I'm sure of it," Geth replied.

"They'll never show their faces as long as you have

this oaf trampling through the fields with you," Zale said, pointing toward Edgar.

"For your information," Clover argued, "Edgar is not an oaf."

"Well, his actions are oafish," Zale clarified. "I am so tired, Geth. You dragged me out of my home to exhaust me to death."

"I've never heard of a prison cell described as home," Geth said, disgusted. "But it might be wise for us to sleep for a moment."

"Remember what happened to us last time we fell asleep in a field?" Clover reminded them.

"So we were tied up," Zale moaned. "At least we got some rest."

"You're quite the warrior," Clover mocked.

"That's enough," Geth insisted, still trying to figure out how to control the overpowering feelings that were messing up the inside of him. "You two sleep and I'll keep watch."

"Perfect," Clover and Zale said simultaneously.

Clover instructed Edgar to smash down some of the crops and clear a hidden spot for them to rest. Edgar gladly trampled down some growth and collapsed on the ground. The massive beast began snoring almost immediately.

"You sure you can stay awake?" Clover asked Geth with a yawn.

"What if I said no?" Geth asked.

"That's nice," Clover replied, not listening any longer and already beginning to doze on top of Edgar.

Clover and Zale both began to breathe in deep sleep as Geth stood looking upward at the clear purple day. He walked around the small trampled area and peered down the rows, looking for any sign of life. Geth cleared his throat and looked toward the fields.

"I know you're out there," he finally said as kindly as he could.

There was nothing but the sound of the witt stalks bending slightly in the wind.

"My name is Geth," Geth informed the crops. "I'm a friend of Eve and Anna."

Clover mumbled something about Phoebe and then turned over and continued to sleep.

"You don't have to come out," Geth told them. "Just let me know I'm not talking to crops."

There was no reply.

"I suppose I have nothing better to do," Geth said, continuing to speak. "I'm from Foo. I'm a lithen. This man on the ground is my brother Zale. The beast is Edgar, and the little guy's a sycophant from Foo."

One of the stalks sounded as if it were holding in

a sneeze. The noise gave Geth some incentive to keep talking.

"We need your help," Geth pleaded. "We were traveling with Anna, but she was captured. We are looking for Lars, to enlist his help."

There was the definite sound of whispering now. Geth knew whoever was whispering was trying to make it sound like wind, but he clearly heard the word *Anna*.

"Can you at least let us know where Lars is?" Geth asked. "I was told he is the one I should talk to."

"We're not in the habit of trusting others," a voice said from behind Geth.

Geth spun around, and there was a woman wearing a sparkly dress with a crown on her head. Geth had seen a lot of beauty pageants while living in Reality. As a tree standing outside of Terry and Addy's window, he had been forced to witness a lot of bad TV—of course, had he not seen what he had, he would have been unfamiliar with the look and probably would have thought that the girl standing in front of him was a queen. But Geth knew that somewhere in Reality some young girl had dreamed long and hard about being a beauty pageant queen, and her dream had ended up here.

"Hello," Geth said, looking straight at the woman's blue eyes. "I'm Geth."

"We heard you," she said.

"I'm from—"

"Listen," the woman interrupted, "this is a relatively small realm. News of you has traveled far. We received word a day ago that you were captured by Payt. Now here you are standing in our fields."

"I was captured," Geth said. "But we escaped."

"That's not possible," she said with poise. "Payt kills or controls all he captures."

"I'm right here," Geth pointed out. "Am I allowed to know your name?"

"Nicole," she said, revealing not only her name but the name of the child who had dreamt her up. "I enjoy spending time with family, summer sports, and helping children learn how to read."

"That's great," Geth said. "Do you know Anna?"

"Of course," Nicole said, smiling while answering the question. "Anna's goals are dancing with a real New York dance troupe and being the first ballerina in space. Here in Zendor she hides like the rest of us women. Anna and Eve kept the order in their area."

"Eve was captured," Geth said, realizing that Nicole responded like a pageant contestant to questions. "Payt has control of her."

"Eve was a believer in things she had no real understanding of," Nicole said. "She would never have won Miss Congeniality. I heard that she traveled to Foo and survived the return. How is that possible?"

"I'm not completely familiar with the laws of Zendor," Geth admitted. "I know you can't survive long in Foo. Eve wasn't there long before the boors brought us back."

"We are no more committed to helping you than Anna was," Nicole said.

"That's encouraging," Geth replied. "Anna had agreed to help us shortly before she was taken. She said she could take us to Stone Holders who would know how to get to Lars. Can you help?"

"It is my goal to help as many less fortunate people as I can," Nicole said, smiling. "I feel that all people should help other people to be the best they can be. As for helping you now? No."

Geth rubbed his forehead and ran his hand quickly though his hair. He tried to compose himself, but he was beginning to feel sick from all the uncertainty inside of him.

"Listen," Geth said, letting some of his disgust bleed out, "I'm not sure who here is worth saving. Don't any of you want to be free? Don't you want lives?"

"Yes," Nicole said. "I dream of a world where everyone has lives like we do. Because if we didn't have a life, how else could we be here?"

"Sure," Geth said. "You exist. Bookends exist, but they don't live. Will you at least point me to where I might find this Lars?"

"No," Nicole said, still smiling. "But if you let me go change into my bathing suit, I'll be ready for that portion of the competition."

"That's not necessary," Geth said, exasperated. He turned to yell at the fields, "Is there anyone here that will help?"

Nicole smiled. "I firmly believe that's a no."

"That's not true," a voice hollered back from twenty feet into the field.

"Quiet, Jill," Nicole insisted. "This is my time."

Jill stepped out from between the stalks of witt. She was a tall girl with round glasses; a colorful sweater was tied around her neck. She had short brown hair and was wearing a pleated skirt with white knee socks. Geth wasn't completely sure what sort of dream she was.

"I will not be quiet," Jill insisted. "I have things to say."

"Jill's new here," Nicole complained.

"If you think ten years is new," Jill complained. "I

always want to do something exciting, but all we do is hide and talk about cute Stone Holders."

"So can you lead me to Lars?" Geth asked.

"No, but I can show you where there are some Stone Holders," she bragged. "They'll take you to Lars."

"That would be great," Geth said thankfully.

"You shouldn't get involved," Nicole argued with poise.

"Who cares?" Jill whined. "I can't take it anymore. I'm so bored."

"Perfect," Geth called out. "Are there any others that are bored?"

Slowly a few other women emerged from the fields. One of the women looked like an old-fashioned airplane pilot with a leather helmet and a scarf. Another woman was wearing a leotard and feathery gloves.

"We too are bored," the airplane pilot said defiantly. "Do you have a plane?"

"No," Geth said, sincerely sorry. "But we have Edgar."

Everyone looked at Edgar as he lay there with Clover sleeping on top of him.

"I can't fly that," the woman complained.

"That won't be necessary," Geth said, the sudden

optimism of volunteers causing any anger he felt to wane.

Geth filled them in on what had happened and what was going to happen. Nicole kept trying to tell them all how foolish they were, but the boredom and depression of hiding for years made them all eager to at least try to be brave. Altogether there were twelve female volunteers willing to march with Geth. There had been sixteen, but when Geth had explained in detail about what had happened to Anna and the others, four had simply backed out and disappeared into the fields.

After they were all on the same page, Geth walked over and woke up Clover. He shook the little sycophant as he slept on top of Edgar. Clover woke up mumbling.

"I know, and I shaved just yesterday," Clover said with his eyes still closed. "More like a four o'clock shadow, wouldn't you say?"

"Wake up," Geth said firmly. "Clover."

Clover's blue eyes flashed open. He looked at Geth as if he were a confusing illusion. He rubbed his eyes with his fists and breathed in deeply. Clover yawned and blinked a few times while looking around. Edgar and Zale were still sleeping, but Geth was standing there surrounded by a cluster of strange women.

"Really?" Clover said, disgusted. "I go to sleep for a few minutes and wake up to find you with a bunch of new girlfriends?"

"Girlfriends," four of the girls giggled, liking the sound of what Clover had said.

"I'm worried that Phoebe might not be okay with this," Clover added.

"Who's Phoebe?" one of the girls demanded of Geth. "What was all that girlfriend talk?"

"That's not important," Geth said seriously. "We need to get moving."

"Not important?" Clover tisked. "Poor Phoebe."

"Just get up," Geth said, not giving Clover's comments a second thought. "These girls are going to help. Wake up, Zale."

Geth lightly kicked Zale's left shoulder as he lay on the ground in a deep sleep. Zale complained for a few moments and then sat up. Edgar, on the other hand, wouldn't wake up. Geth and Jill tried to shake him awake, but the big Tangle just wouldn't move.

"He was pretty tired," Clover said. "Try pinching him."

Jill pinched Geth.

"Not him," Clover scolded. "Edgar."

"Of course," Jill said, blushing. "Actually, I'm not pinching that thing."

"Wait a second," Clover said, reaching into the void on his robe. "I think I have something that might help."

Clover fished around in his void for a few seconds and then pulled out the broken arm of a Barbie.

"That's not it," Clover said, smiling.

Everyone stared at him and the dismembered Barbie arm.

"What?" Clover said defensively. "I found this near Leven's old home. It makes a perfect back scratcher." Clover reached back with the plastic arm and scratched his own back. "See?"

Clover put the arm back into his void and continued to rummage around. He pulled out an old cassette tape of Hanukkah songs, a used toothbrush in the shape of a pencil, two packs of crackers, a dead butterfly, a Chinese takeout menu, and a deflated balloon.

"What are you looking for?" Geth asked.

"Remember when we were in Foo," Clover said, "and I had to help Leven hide our ride with that vapor stick?"

Geth shook his head.

"Oh, yeah, you wouldn't remember," Clover said, hitting his forehead with the back of his left palm. "You were there, but you weren't there. That was the time I had put you in my void."

Geth shivered at the memory.

"Anyhoo," Clover said, still rummaging. "I think a vapor stick could help now. I just need to find . . . here it is." Clover pulled out a short, dark stick. "All I need to do is—"

"No!" Geth yelled.

"What?" Clover asked.

"I might have been in your void, but I remember Leven complaining for weeks about the smell that thing made," Geth said, agitated.

"Leven has a really sensitive nose," Clover waved. "But I was there, and I don't recall it being that bad."

"I think we've had enough smell with those noble-berries," Geth said, referring to the melons they had cracked open in their prisons. "Let's not have—"

Before Geth could say any more, Clover broke the stick and waved it beneath Edgar's nose. Edgar just lay there, but as the smell began to drip from the stick, the poor beast flinched. Edgar's huge, silvery eyes popped open, and a look of complete panic flashed across them. Edgar reeled his head back and scrambled up onto his feet as the crops nearest him began to wither from the odor.

The smell drifted up to Clover.

The small hairs on Clover's nose curled and began to melt. The little sycophant tried to act like it was no big deal, but he couldn't even breathe for fear of his nostrils exploding.

The smell hit Geth and the rest of them like a wave. Nicole passed out with a little wave good-bye as Jill and the others began running.

"Fo . . . ll . . . ow me," Jill choked out.

"What have you done?" Geth yelled, the smell filling his mouth as he spoke. "That's worse than the berries."

"I didn't . . ." Clover began to sway under the influence of the smell.

"I can taste it," Geth said frantically.

Edgar and Zale took off after Jill as Clover leapt up toward Geth's right shoulder. The smell was paralyzing. Clover passed out mid jump. He fell to the ground in a small, fuzzy heap. Geth had his nose plugged with one hand and reached down for Clover with his other, as more and more stalks of witt withered and bent over in repugnant defeat.

Geth spat and coughed violently as he ran after the others.

Crops were dropping like thin corpses as the smell radiated like a slow-moving explosion from the spot where Clover had dropped the stick. Geth could feel heat and stench pushing up on the back of his neck as he ran. He kept his nose plugged and held Clover by the ankles.

Edgar held Zale in his arms and was ripping through the field at a terrific pace with Jill and the other girls right behind him. It took a good mile of distance for the smell to no longer be a problem. They stopped momentarily to catch their breath and spit the taste out of their mouths.

"I've never smelled anything like that," Jill said, repulsed.

Edgar growled.

"Where'd that sycophant get that?" Zale complained.

"Foo," Geth said.

"That's how Foo smells?" Jill asked with concern.

"No," Geth replied, trying to gently shake Clover back into consciousness.

Clover mumbled and opened his eyes slowly. He looked at Geth and the others and shook his head while pounding on his right ear with his right palm. Clover licked his lips and winced.

"What happened?" he said, smacking his lips. "And what's that taste?"

"You happened," Geth said, trying to spit the taste out of his own mouth. "A vapor stick? Where did you get that?"

"Oh yeah," Clover said, remembering what he had done. "The Eggmen had some rotten candy. They didn't want it to go to waste, so they made those sticks."

"What use does that have?" Zale asked, disgusted.

"Smell can be a great motivator," Clover said as he pulled his nostrils open and blew out.

"No more vapor sticks, Clover," Geth insisted.

"Right," Clover insisted back.

Geth turned to Jill, who was standing there with only three other women.

"Where are the rest?" Geth asked.

"The smell sort of changed their minds," Jill said. "They felt stinky was worse than bored."

Clover looked at Geth and tilted his head as if studying his friend's face.

"Wait a second," Clover said curiously. "Are you getting frustrated?"

"No," Geth lied. "Let's keep going."

"Come with me," Jill said kindly.

Jill held out her right hand and Geth took it. She smiled wide as the other three woman steamed in jealously. Jill pulled Geth through the field with purpose. The airplane pilot reached out for Zale's hand. Zale looked at her and grimaced.

"I can walk myself," he insisted.

Clover jumped up on Edgar's head, and everyone filed down the thick row of witt, following after Geth and Jill. Edgar and Clover took up the rear. Edgar's large shoulders and body pushed the stalks aside like a heavy comb parting grassy hair. Clover looked down at Edgar and smiled.

"I wish you could talk," he said, patting Edgar.

"I wish you'd stop talking," Zale butted in.

Clover disappeared and they all hiked on.

## Chapter Thirteen

# DAYLIGHT
# FADING

**W**isdom is a tricky trait. There are so many these days who profess to be wise when they are no more intelligent than most tree bark. Knowing how to coupon doesn't make you a genius, it makes you a spendthrift who can operate scissors. Knowing how to type doesn't make you brilliant, it makes you a type A-through-Z personality. Likewise, knowing how to Sudoku doesn't make you intellectually superior, it simply means that you not only think in the box but you think in the little boxes. Wisdom comes from living and learning. I know how to speak to an eagle because I spent two weeks high on a mountain tied to a tree and having to learn to live with a nest full of hungry raptors. I can speak seven languages because I have been kidnapped and retrained by seven very different nationalities. And I am wise beyond my years because I once had to boil and eat an entire set of encyclopedias to survive while being held captive by a librarian.

There are very few words that I have not literally devoured.

Geth followed closely behind Jill. It had taken a couple of miles for him to finally shake his hand free from hers as she pulled him. At first Geth had tried to be kind about it, but eventually it was necessary for him to stop and yank back as hard as he could. The moment his mitt was free, one of the women behind him tried to reach out for it. Geth clasped both his hands in front of him to keep them away.

"Let's just walk," Geth insisted. "I think I'll be okay without holding someone's hand."

The woman sighed in disappointment. Jill tried to make a case for how she would feel more comfortable if Geth at least held onto her elbow as they walked, but then Geth made a case for how that would never happen.

"We could carry you," one of the athletic women marching behind Geth offered.

"Yes," the female pilot said. "Let's carry him."

"No carrying," Geth insisted.

Their party moved through thick fields. Hidden

by the growth, they had no fear of being spotted by any boors. But, hidden by the growth, their world began to feel claustrophobic and depressing. And as darkness came on, their journey felt so heavy it was hard to keep walking.

The fields eventually came to an end at a small dirt road near the base of a tall mountain range. Once they had stopped moving, the air was silent.

"So where is this Lars from here?" Geth whispered.

"Not far," Jill whispered back. "You and I could go look for him alone."

"I thought you didn't know where he was," Geth reminded her.

"I don't," Jill admitted. "I just thought we could go looking. You'll need a Stone Holder now."

Jill walked out of the crops and onto the dirt road. She held a glow stone in her palm and opened and closed her fingers to make the stone blink. Seconds later there were lights flashing back at her in the distance. Jill opened and closed her hand some more and the lights began to move closer.

The distant lights grew brighter and brighter until they were two soft blue lights standing directly in front of them. Inside of those glowing spheres were two Stone Holders. One was a cowboy; the other was dressed like a soccer player.

"Howdy, Jill," the cowboy said, obviously familiar with her. "What brings you to our neck of the woods?"

Clover grumbled, bothered by the folksy talk.

"These men need help, Nick," she said. "This is Geth; the one back there with the uneven beard is Zale. They're lithens."

"Well, I'll be," Nick whistled. "I ain't seen the likes of you in our parts before."

"Seriously?" Clover complained. "Does he have to talk like that?"

"Hello," Geth said, ignoring Clover. "We need to speak to someone named Lars."

"I am Diego," the soccer player said proudly, kicking his feet as he said it. "Lars does not speak to just anyone."

"Well, if you'll take us, we can find out if he'll speak to me," Geth said.

Nick and Diego whispered to each other for a few moments. Nick finally turned around.

"How do we know you're not boors?" Nick asked. "You know, a wolf in sheep's clothing."

"We're not boors," Geth said sternly. "It's dark and we're moving. Aside from that, you'll have to take our word for it."

"A man's word is good enough for me," Nick insisted. "Besides, you've got a real trusting face."

"Doesn't he?" Jill said dreamily.

"What's the little and big creature?" Diego asked. "Their faces are not so trusting."

"This is Clover," Geth answered. "He's a sycophant from Foo. The big guy's Edgar. He's a Tangle."

"There's talk of a Tangle beyond the wall that guards Pencilbottom Castle," Nick said suspiciously. "I've not heard of the beast being anywhere else."

"Well," Clover said proudly, "this is that same Tangle. Edgar. We saved him from Payt."

Nick whistled a long whistle of approval.

Nick and Diego looked at each other. Nick shrugged and Diego did some fancy soccer steps with his feet.

"I believe Lars will insist on seeing you," Diego said. "And you should have no problem with the air."

"Diego's right," Nick said. "So we'll take you, but the critters stay here."

"You shouldn't call women *critters,*" Clover said indignantly. "Wait, is he talking about me?"

"They'll stay here," Geth agreed, ignoring Clover. "There isn't time to waste."

"Way to defend my honor," Clover complained.

"Let's go," Geth said, impatient to leave.

"The women needn't come as well," Nick said. "Lars doesn't exactly trust the fairer sex. Sorry, Jill."

"His loss," Jill said flirtatiously. "We'll be waiting, Geth."

Jill tried to lean in and give Geth a kiss good-bye, but she wasn't quick enough before the Stone Holders led Geth and Zale into the dark.

The four women slipped between the stalks and disappeared. Clover tried to act sad and neglected, but the truth was that both he and Edgar were pretty excited about the opportunity to sleep some more.

"What say you lie down and I sleep on your back?" Clover asked Edgar.

Having a snout made it difficult to smile, but somehow Edgar managed.

Clover lay on Edgar's back. He fidgeted for a few moments and then got back up.

"I just remembered that I have a quick errand to run," Clover said. "I'll be right back."

Edgar was too asleep to respond.

✦ Chapter Fourteen ✦

# HOPE IS LIKE
# THE WIND

Being separated from those you love or feel safe around can be scary. I can remember my thirteenth birthday when I lost my entire family. I found them a few hours later when I got home from school, but still those few hours we were separated were frightening. Nobody enjoys having to part ways with those they depend on. There aren't many greeting cards that celebrate the magic of being abandoned.

"Congratulations, you've been left by the wayside."

Nope, card companies, like most of us, have figured out that having to be separated is something not to celebrate but to commiserate.

Geth and Clover were separated at the moment, and although Geth wasn't wishing he had a card to

138

celebrate it with, he was doing just fine. Of course, he was a lithen, and separation was simply another moment in fate's master plan.

Nick and Diego were fast walkers. The speed suited Geth. Zale, on the other hand, would have preferred a slightly more casual stroll.

"Come on," Geth challenged his brother.

"I haven't walked this much in years," Zale complained. "I am conditioned to sit."

"We'll change that," Geth said proudly. "Come on."

The Stone Holders led them into a thin tunnel that sloped upward. Candles were hanging on the walls, making it unnecessary to use glow stones any longer.

"This realm baffles me," Geth said to Zale as they walked. "So much work has been put into hiding. What could have been accomplished if you had led these people to put their efforts toward crushing Payt?"

"Don't lecture me," Zale insisted. "I have coped how I could."

"We weren't raised to use the word *cope*," Geth reminded Zale. "We were born to surpass."

"I like how you talk," Nick said, turning his head to join the conversation as they walked. "I don't think I was dreamt up to hide in a cave. Some little pardner named Nick dreamt me up to be something bigger than he is. I bet that kid ain't hiding in a cave."

"Wow," Geth said with surprise. "You're the first person I've heard talk some sense here."

"He is a fool," Diego pointed out. "Everyone knows that Nick is touched in the head. But we like him. He makes us feel better about ourselves."

"What he's saying isn't foolish," Geth scolded. "You're the creations of someone wanting more. Maybe fate is wise to cut you off from them and leave you here. It seems as if you're all content to be just what you are and nothing else."

"Yes," Diego said. "Now you talk the sense."

"No," Nick snapped. "You don't get it. He's reminding us that we should be more."

"He's doing nothing but spitting out lithen doctrine," Zale explained. "My brother's intentions might be good, but he has no idea what a month, a year, decades here can do to a person's mind and ability to see hope as the errant dog that it is."

"There's the opening," Nick said happily.

All four of them moved through the tunnel and into a new cave. From there they took stairs that ran downward and looked to have no ending.

"How do you know where you're going?" Geth asked.

"Spend a few years moving through these tunnels and I'm certain you'll know your way," Nick said. "There used to just be a few tunnels leading to the valley of Lars, but now there are hundreds that connect. I still get lost on occasion, but there are hubs and rooms to recognize all over. I always just make my way back to some spot I know and hope . . ." Nick looked firmly at Diego. "And hope that my mind ain't so confused as to not get me out."

"Great," Zale complained. "We're being led around by someone with a soft brain."

The stairs grew dark as the candles burning on the wall ran out.

"Just keep moving," Nick said. "The stairs still go on for a spell. Seconds before Zale was about to sit down and refuse to go any further, a pinpoint of light could be seen in the far distance.

"We can take you to the light," Nick said. "From there you're on your own."

"Perfect," Geth said gratefully.

"Perfect?" Zale scoffed. "You could really use a dictionary. I think your definition of perfection is a bit skewed."

The pinpoint of weak light slowly grew larger. At first it looked like they were heading toward a glow stone, but as they moved closer, they could see that the light was clearer and brighter than that.

The stairs came to a stop at the end of a tunnel that opened up looking over a bright valley filled with grass and trees. The sun was just coming up, but Geth could see a thick blue river running through the deep, rich grasses and there were birds flying through a sky that was as clear and glossy as glass.

At the end of the tunnel and stairs there was a brick balcony with a stone railing that overlooked the beautiful landscape below. There was also a large telescope on the balcony. The telescope was pointing downward as if it were waiting for tourists who wanted to take a closer look at what lay below.

The view was definitely worth looking at.

The valley was completely surrounded by mountains so tall that Geth couldn't see the tops of them. Light clouds slid through the glassy sky as a soothing wind drifted up and around them. All over the sides of the mountains Geth could see other balconies where other tunnels were.

The fields below were peppered with horses and other animals that Geth couldn't instantly recognize. In the center of the valley was a small hill thick with forested growth. On the top of the hill was a cluster of massive trees.

The smell of grass and sunshine filled the air.

Geth stood there with his mouth open, baffled by the utter beauty and surprise of the scene before him.

"What is this place?" Geth whispered reverently.

"Lars Valley," Nick said. "Purdy, ain't it?"

"I don't understand," Geth uttered, looking around. "Are there boors here?"

"No," Nick said solemnly. "Boors know nothing of this place. They can't travel through the tunnels due to the darkness."

"It's so peaceful," Zale said, dumbfounded.

"Where's Lars?" Geth asked.

"In the middle of the valley," Nick said, pointing. "Up in the growth of the trees."

"You can't take us?" Geth asked.

"No," Nick insisted. "The air will kill us Stone Holders. It might kill you, but I'm guessing since you're not a dream you'll be fine."

"Aren't you standing in the air right now?" Geth asked, confused. "You look fine."

"Oh, that," Nick said, waving. "Lars said that the air on the balconies is perfectly safe, seeing how it's still kind of tunnel air."

Zale stared at Nick as if he were an idiot.

"Does that make sense to you?" Zale asked in disbelief.

"It's not best to question Lars," Diego insisted. "We are fine in the caves."

"I need to talk to Lars," Geth said with purpose. "I hope he's not too surprised by visitors."

"He won't be surprised," Nick said. "He watches from those trees. He most likely already knows you're about. Nothing surprises Lars."

Nick stepped up to the telescope and directed it toward the hill in the center of the valley. He looked into the telescope.

"He's not on the platform," Nick said. "But I bet he's watching from inside the leaves."

"Let's find out," Geth said passionately. "Come on, Zale."

Geth and Zale hopped over the balcony railing and fell the twenty feet down onto the green, grassy pasture below. Geth tumbled and ended up on his knees. Zale tumbled and ended up on his rear. Geth stood up and helped his brother do the same. The two of them looked back and up and waved at Nick and Diego on the balcony. As soon as they were clearly out of earshot, Zale spoke.

"What was that garbage about the air being unbreathable?" Zale asked Geth.

"Just that," Geth answered. "Garbage. I'm interested to see what this Lars is up to."

Geth began to run down the field of green grass with Zale behind him. He wove through a thick stretch of tall white trees with red leaves, breathing in deeply. His lungs didn't burn, and the muscles in his legs grew stronger with each step. There was a wide stream flowing quickly with amber-colored water. Geth walked across a big stone bridge that spanned it. He then climbed up the bank on the other side and waited for his brother.

When Zale finally caught up, there was a curious mix of confusion and serenity on his face.

"What is this place?" Zale said. "The air's not poisonous. In fact, I feel stronger just breathing it."

"It's remarkable," Geth agreed.

"It's a slap in the face to everyone who has suffered the crushing blah of Zendor," Zale ranted. "It's a slap in the face to me. How dare this be kept from others?"

Geth looked toward the hill in the center of the valley.

"My mind doesn't feel so sleepy," Zale added.

"That's a good thing," Geth reminded him.

The two lithens looked around, breathing in deeply.

"You know you left me for dead," Zale finally said. "I've been rotting in that cell for years."

"We had no idea you were alive," Geth answered innocently.

"Really?" Zale complained. "On the words of others, you accepted my death?"

"The reports seemed sincere," Geth said solemnly. "Had I thought for a moment that you lived, I would have torn apart Foo."

"Yet you didn't think for a moment," Zale reminded him.

"I had to accept the fate," Geth said honestly. "Your death wasn't easy on any of us."

"I didn't die," Zale argued. "But you were more than willing to write me off."

"That's not true," Geth said firmly. "We have not written you off. Even in death we knew we would meet again. My question is, why didn't you fight to return?"

"You think I didn't fight?" Zale spat. "You think I was thrown in here by Sabine and that I instantly decided to fold and give up? I fought, Geth. I fought and fought to convince these stupid creatures to want more for themselves. There were a few, but they were captured and killed as quickly as they came forward to fight. I could find no exit from Zendor, and in my eagerness to destroy Payt, I was captured. I walked right into one of his traps. He didn't even have the mercy to kill me. He let me and my brain rot for all these years."

"Your life is not over," Geth pointed out carefully.

"I have nothing," Zale said. "You question why I don't want to fight? Well, there's nothing for me to return to, no life to step back into. I am dead to everyone who ever knew me."

"That's pathetic," Geth said honestly. "I don't care if you have been caged up for fifty years; you know what your course in this world is. You are a lithen. You were dealt a hand that should now be an experience to make you stronger, not a weight to keep pulling you under. At what point is it okay to give in and let the evil of others wash over and drown you?"

"You're preachy," Zale said. "That sycophant's right, you've always used way too many words."

Geth hit Zale as hard as he could under the chin, using a bit of his brawn instead of his brain. Zale flew back and against a tree. He slid to the ground and grabbed his jaw while moaning.

"I don't remember you hitting people so much," Zale said.

"I don't remember needing to," Geth replied.

"I'm your older brother," Zale argued.

"I find that hard to believe at times," Geth said. "My older brother was a man of great conviction and character. A person who would do what is right at all costs and regardless of how he had been treated or if the outcome might harm him."

Zale was quiet for a few moments as he stared at the tips of his bare feet. He looked up at Geth.

"We're going to die," Zale said.

"Everyone dies," Geth reminded him.

"That's the first sensible thing I've heard you say," Zale said sarcastically.

Geth left Zale to cool down a bit and get control of his own emotions. He walked back down to the amber river. Geth kneeled by the water and cupped his hands. He took a couple of drinks and splashed water on his face and arms. He then dunked his head under. Back up, he pushed his wet hair behind his ears. His blue eyes shone under the bright sun. Geth shook his hands dry and stared up at the clear sky.

"This place might be even prettier than Foo," Clover said while invisible and to the left of Geth.

Geth shook his head. "Somehow I knew you wouldn't stay put."

"See?" Clover said. "So in a way I'm just doing what I'm expected to. I guess I'm reliable."

"Among other things," Geth said, trying not to sound happy. "How long have you been here?"

"The whole time," Clover admitted. "I was riding

on that cowboy who led you here. I thought it would make me feel western."

"Did it?"

"No," Clover said sadly. "And his hat stank."

"What about Edgar?" Geth asked. "You were supposed to keep an eye on him. He needs you."

"He's fine," Clover insisted. "I told the girls to look after him. Besides, he doesn't need me like you do. Now, what is this place?"

Geth stood up and looked around slowly. All over, colorful rivers flowed and deep, rich fields of grass and growth swayed mesmerizingly in the wind.

"I'm not sure what this place is, but it's amazing," Geth admitted. "Breathe in deep."

Clover took a giant swig of air.

"It feels nice in my nostrils," Clover said sincerely. "I heard you and Zale talking about the air. I like it."

"But for some reason nobody but Lars lives here."

"Maybe everyone's allergic to pretty?" Clover suggested. "I mean, some of the people we've met out there are sort of ragged and dirty."

"I don't think people are allergic to pretty," Geth insisted. "They've just had to live in caves and fields. I can't think of a reason why they don't just come here. The whole realm could fit in this valley."

"Maybe Lars doesn't like to share."

"Maybe," Geth replied.

"Listen," Clover said seriously. "Not to change the subject, but I have something to say about Zale. I heard what you two were arguing about a few minutes ago. I know he's your big brother, but I just think you should remember that I don't always get along with my brothers."

"I'm sorry to hear that," Geth said.

"No," Clover waved. "This isn't about me. Besides, my brothers think they know so much more just because they're older. I knew that fire would be hot; I just wanted to touch it to make sure. They're not the boss of me."

"You showed them," Geth said supportively.

"Right," Clover agreed. "Okay, so I had to wear that bandage for a few months, but I'm my own sycophant."

"Sure," Geth agreed.

"Actually," Clover said with a sigh, "I can see now why you don't get along with Zale. Brothers are the worst. I wish I was an only child."

"You're the only child I see here," Geth said comfortingly.

"Thanks," Clover replied, reading the teasing as a compliment and not stopping to realize that he wasn't even visible at the moment.

Geth began to walk back toward the direction where Zale was.

"Wait," Geth asked Clover as he was walking. "Are you hugging me?"

There was a long pause before Clover replied, "Maybe."

Geth reached up and petted the invisible sycophant on his left shoulder.

"Who needs older brothers when they've got a lithen," Clover bragged.

"And Zale's got nothing on you," Geth said back.

"Well, he is taller," Clover pointed out.

"There is that," Geth said, laughing.

Geth and Clover found Zale still leaning against the tree with his eyes closed. Instead of nudging him, the two of them decided to sit down and take a few minutes to lean themselves. The valley was so beautiful, and the air so comforting as they breathed, that the aches and pains of what they had been through washed off of them and they drifted quickly to sleep.

## Chapter Fifteen

# PERFECTION
# AT A PRICE

K nowing what to trust isn't easy. I trust that most bridges will do their job, but I've been on one that was not only rickety but untrustworthy. As I fell hundreds of feet down into the alligator-infested water below, I realized that trust is earned. I would have spoken very highly of that bridge had it held up, but now I simply have to trust that alligators will always find me a bit chewy and leave me alone. What to trust? We trust that the sun will come up, but everyone knows that the moon is far less reliable. We trust that the future will bring innovation, but can we trust our shady past not to ruin things? We trust that soda will always be fizzy, bees will always buzz, and pickles will always make you pucker. Added to that list is my trust for

Geth. Sure, the merging with the Ezra half hasn't been easy, but I trust that in the end Geth will do what he needs to do when he needs to do it. Otherwise, there will simply be an end, and I trust that nobody will be happy about that.

I trust you understand.

Geth woke with a start. Clover was sitting on the ground in front of him chewing on what looked like a stick of yellow wax.

"How long was I out?" Geth asked, looking over at Zale, who was still sleeping against the tree.

"About thirty minutes," Clover answered while chewing.

"What are you eating?" Geth questioned, closing his eyes to rest a couple of seconds more.

"I'm not sure," Clover replied. "I was hungry so I just fished around in my void. This smelled better than some of the other things in there."

Geth's eyes flashed open.

"You're not supposed to just eat things you find in there," Geth scolded. "We've been over this."

"I know you and Leven have something against candy," Clover complained. "But I'm perfectly fine. See?"

Clover held out his arms to show Geth that nothing was happening to him.

"Not all of the food in my void causes problems," Clover continued. "Remember that cake thing I saved from Reality?"

"The Twinkie?" Geth asked.

"Yeah," Clover smiled. "What a great name. It didn't do anything."

"It made you sick," Geth reminded him.

"It didn't do anything cool," Clover clarified. "Some food is just food. Now, do you want the last bite of this? It's really good."

Clover reached out and tried to hand Geth the final bit of the yellow, waxy stuff.

"I'll pass," Geth said, trying to shake the feelings of sleep out of his head. "We need to get Zale up and keep going."

Clover popped the last bit of food into his mouth and then jumped on Geth as he stood up. Geth nudged Zale's right foot with his left foot.

"Zale," Geth said. "Get up."

Zale didn't stir in the least.

"Hold on," Clover said, leaping down onto Zale's chest. "I think I have an alarm clock." Clover reached into his void and pulled out an iPhone. He tried to turn it on, but it was long dead. "I used to see everyone using these in Reality," he said, perplexed. "It's like an

154

alarm clock that also tells people what to do if they talk into it."

Geth looked down at Clover.

"This one won't even turn on," Clover complained.

Geth stared at the dead iPhone.

"Even if that did turn on, it wouldn't work here," Geth said, waking up more with each word he spoke.

"What's the use of it, then?" Clover asked. "It's just a fancy rock."

Clover threw the phone up into the air to get rid of it. The phone flew up, twisted, and fell straight back down. It hit Zale squarely on the forehead.

"Ouch!"

"Your brother's up," Clover told Geth casually. "I guess it's not that bad an alarm clock after all."

Zale rubbed his head and looked around in bewilderment.

"Let's go," Geth instructed him.

Clover sprang from Zale to Geth and settled in on Geth's right shoulder. Zale stood up, stretched, cursed a little more, and began to walk after them.

"So we're heading to that hill in the middle of the valley?" Clover asked.

Geth nodded.

"And this Lars fellow is good?" Clover questioned.

"Everyone seems to think so."

Clover bounced from off of Geth and onto Zale.

"Do you mind?" Zale complained.

"Not at all," Clover insisted, thinking that Zale was commenting on the fact that Clover had to sit on Zale's bony shoulder. "Listen, what do you know about this Lars?"

"I've heard his name mentioned on occasion," Zale replied, still bothered that Clover was on him. "Last I was in Foo, sycophants were not supposed to sit on shoulders without permission."

"I know," Clover said with relief. "I'm just as happy as you that times have changed. So what have you heard about Lars?"

"I didn't hear much down in my cell," Zale grumbled. "Just years of beautiful solitude. But there has been mention of this Lars and that some of these Stone Holders and women in Zendor think he's wise. Payt loathes him and thinks he's a joke."

"I like jokes," Clover said innocently.

Clover leapt back to Geth.

"Hey, toothpick," Clover said casually. "Do you think . . . um . . ."

"Do I think um?" Geth asked, beginning to walk faster as he and Zale shook off all traces of sleep.

"Well, actually . . ." Clover disappeared.

"Are you okay?" Geth asked.

There was a long pause followed by a soft gasp.

"Listen," Geth said seriously. "It makes me uncomfortable to have you gasping so soon after eating something from your void."

"Sorry," Clover said, his voice filled with concern.

"So are you okay?" Geth asked. "Show yourself."

"Just keep walking," Clover said frantically.

"What's happening?" Zale asked from behind Geth.

"Clover ate something that's not sitting well with him."

"What'd he eat?" Zale asked.

"He doesn't know," Geth replied.

"Actually, I remember now," Clover said sadly. "It was candy."

"What kind of candy?" Zale asked. "I haven't had candy in years. It seems like you could have shared."

"You don't want what he's got," Geth insisted.

"What kind of candy was it?" Zale asked, honestly jealous of Clover.

"Wart Wax," Clover moaned.

The sound of something small and popping could be heard.

"They feel weird," Clover panicked.

"What feels weird?" Zale asked.

"The warts," Clover answered.

"Get off!" Geth yelled, brushing at an invisible Clover on his shoulder.

"Hey!" Clover hollered back, jumping onto Zale.

"I think he's on me!" Zale yelled while batting at the air. "Get him off of me!"

"I'm not on you anymore," Clover said, clinging to the front of Geth.

Geth reached forward and grabbed at the air in front of him. His hands closed in on an invisible Clover.

"Is that you?" Geth said, bewildered. "It feels like . . ."

Clover materialized. Geth and Zale screamed in unison.

"Is it bad?" Clover cried.

"It's horrible," Geth yelled back.

Clover looked like a gray, bloated watermelon covered in lumpy warts. His eyes were sunken and surrounded by nubby growths the size of marbles. His fingers and toes were riddled with bumps and bits that stuck out all over. Geth stopped running, stunned, and Zale plowed into the back of him. Clover popped out of Geth's hands and bounced against the ground and back up into the air. Geth was tempted to not even catch him, but his conscience got the best of him and he reached out. He snagged Clover with his left hand and set him on the ground.

"What's happening?" Geth asked, backing away from Clover.

"It's the candy," Clover said. "I remember trying some years ago. I shouldn't have eaten the entire glob, but I didn't know what it was. They itch."

"Serves you right, not sharing your candy," Zale complained.

"Do you hear yourself?" Geth asked in exasperation. "If he had shared, you'd look just as awful."

Clover started to cry harder.

"It's okay," Geth said, calming down. "It'll wear off, right?"

Clover nodded his thick, knobby head. "Eventually."

"Don't cry," Geth said with compassion. "I'm sure the itching will stop soon."

"I'm not crying because of the itching," Clover sniffed. "I'm crying because warts are contagious."

Geth and Zale both stepped back in horror as warts began to pop and expand like hot corn all over their arms and legs. Geth looked down at his limbs and began to scratch. Zale ran in a circle, swatting at his chest and torso.

"Running won't help," Clover insisted as he

scratched violently at all the warts on his own body. "I think I'm starting to ooze!"

Zale paused to scream louder.

Geth sat down on the ground, scratching and tearing at his arms. Clover tried to apologize, but his mouth was so covered with bumps that he could no longer speak clearly.

"Wadda hepps."

"What?" Geth yelled.

"I ting wadda hepps."

"Water helps," Zale screamed, deciphering Clover's words.

Clover took off waddling as fast as he could toward the amber-colored river. Zale became so swollen that his legs popped out from beneath him and he fell to the ground. Geth kicked at his brother and rolled him like a log. All three of them crashed into the water, violently kicking and hitting at one another. Clover went under and popped up, gasping for air. Zale got caught under Geth as Geth tried to swim with swollen arms and legs.

"Iffing!" Zale yelled.

"Wraveeet!" Geth yelled back.

The cold water washed over them all, soothing their condition and rapidly reversing the swelling. The three of them went floating downstream, holding onto one another and trying to get their bearings. The river grew calm as all three of them returned to normal and drifted downriver. As soon as Zale could speak clearly, he looked pointedly at Clover.

"You should have shared," he said, spitting river water out of his mouth as he spoke. "I would have at least gotten something out of this."

Clover climbed up onto Geth's head looking almost back to normal—soaking wet, but back to normal.

"Sorry," Clover tried to apologize.

"You're cleaning that pocket out," Geth said seriously as the water got swifter. "There are some things in there that should never be used."

"I suppose it wouldn't hurt to take inventory of what's in here," Clover said, patting his robe. "But I'm not throwing out everything."

Geth tried to turn and begin swimming toward the shore, but the water was now moving too fast to swim against.

The three of them hit up against a large, smooth rock in the middle of the river. They twisted around it and shot farther downstream. Up ahead there were more rocks sticking out of the water and blocking their path.

"Where are the Waves when you need them?"

Clover asked, referring to the Waves of the Lime Sea that lived in Foo and guarded the island of Alder.

"Just hold on!" Geth yelled.

They hit against a stone and were twisted around in the water. Geth's body slammed against another rock, and Clover popped off of his head. Clover grabbed at Geth's hair and got just enough to keep from flying off completely.

A third rock jutting out of the river broke up Geth and Zale and sent the brothers to opposite sides of the river. The water became even swifter, and giant fists of foam pounded their heads and roared in their ears. Geth tried to swim, but the water was too strong. Clover looked back and couldn't see anyone.

"Geth!" Clover yelled.

There was no answer.

## Chapter Sixteen

# AMBER WAVES
# OF SANE

I wonder how many of you have ever found yourself trapped in the high branches of a tree. I'd like to think that it is something that happens to everyone. Of course, even if I believed that, I still wouldn't believe that it happens three times to everyone. I don't know how to explain it, but I just have a very difficult time getting out of trees when something with claws and teeth has chased me up one. Yes, being treed is not the most comfortable feeling. There is, however, one scenario where I would love to be stuck in a tree, and that scenario involves a tree house. There's nothing better than a home that has mysteriously settled in the limbs of a tree. It makes every home that has ever been built on the ground look foolish and unambitious.

In conclusion, tree houses are great.

Geth and Zale were pulled from the water by a muscular man with big arms and thin legs. He had a thick mustache that hung over both sides of his mouth like a hairy horseshoe. His head was covered with graying blond hair and he had two deep blue eyes placed perfectly over a long, thin nose.

Geth and Zale had somehow washed up softly onto a sandy bank on the side of the river. They had never had a chance to drown because the river had held them and deposited them without so much as a scratch or a lung full of liquid. The moment they washed up, they were discovered by the man who now was fussing over them. Clover had been clinging to Zale, and as a safety precaution he was keeping invisible and silent.

"The river is like a genie," the man said. "It grants all my wishes."

"You wished for two people to get caught in your net?" Geth asked.

"I wished for you to get caught, Geth," he said. "The fact that your brother is with you is the icing on the cake."

Zale moaned as he lay against the ground. "We almost drowned."

"No," the man insisted. "That river would never allow that."

"You must be Lars," Geth said, coughing.

"Correct," Lars replied. "I saw you enter the valley. I have a great vantage point and a strong telescope. I was wishing for you to make your way to me."

"Your wish wasn't necessary," Geth pointed out. "We came here to find you."

"Still," Lars said, winking. "I prefer to think I wished you here. I also prefer that others think that as well. It's amazing how far a little lore goes in creating an intriguing reputation."

Zale looked confused.

"We're happy we can help add to your reputation," Geth said sincerely.

"Thank you," Lars said. "Now, I must warn you I don't have many visitors, and I get confused sometimes about whether I'm talking to myself or talking to others. Hopefully what I say makes sense."

"Thanks for the warning," Zale said, having the same kind of problems himself.

"But I'm very wise," Lars added.

"That's what we've heard," Geth said. "And obviously confident."

"Sorry," Lars said, confused. "Should I not be so sure of myself? It's just that most of the smart people

I've met in my life are always quick to point out how intelligent they are. I only said that to fit in. I'm trying to be honest with you."

"I appreciate that," Geth said.

"Perfect," Lars cheered.

"You two talk way too much," Zale complained, wringing water out of his dark beard.

"Tell me, Lars, how do you know who we are?" Geth asked, ignoring his brother.

"I have those who inform me," Lars admitted.

"So then you know why we're here?"

"I do," Lars said taking a seat on a stump near Zale. "You wish to rally the troops. Return of the lithens and all that stuff. How exciting. You'll rescue us all."

"It doesn't look like you're too hard up," Zale observed, opening his eyes all the way and joining the conversation.

"Ah," Lars said happily. "And you're Zale—Payt's most famous prisoner—a lithen that gave up."

Zale's nostrils flared, but otherwise he didn't move.

"How do you know so much?" Geth asked curiously.

"Every tunnel that leads into this valley brings news and information that I use to my advantage," Lars said. "I'd be happy to tell you more, but I must insist that we continue this conversation in my home. It will add greatly to my legend to have had lithens as guests. Now, where's your sycophant?"

Geth and Zale stared at Lars.

"The fuzzy thing I saw you arguing with," Lars clarified. "I must say I am most curious about meeting him. I know so little about the silly creatures."

Geth could feel an invisible Clover squeezing his neck to let him know he was there.

"Who knows?" Geth said, trying to act callous. "That particular sycophant is a pest. The river probably consumed him."

"And you don't care?" Lars asked.

"Sycophants are like rats," Zale added.

Lars shrugged. "I suppose you should know about rats, having spent so much time in the dungeons."

Lars stood up and helped Geth to his feet. Geth then helped Zale, and the three of them walked toward the center of the valley. Lars kept a good twenty-foot lead.

"I don't trust him," Zale whispered to Geth.

"Good," Geth whispered back. "I don't either."

Clover squeezed Geth's neck to let him know that he too found Lars to be less than trustworthy.

"So, Lars," Geth called out as they all walked, "are you the only one who lives in this valley?"

"Yes," Lars answered, motioning for them to walk faster. "This is my home."

"The whole place?" Zale said, disgusted.

"I discovered it," Lars said. "No Stone Holders or women among Those Who Hide live here. Can you imagine? If I let one live here, a thousand more would demand I let them come too."

"So the air is fit for them to breathe?" Geth said, growing upset.

"Of course," Lars said. "It's the same air as in every other part of Zendor. Just because the mountains surrounding me reach the clouds doesn't mean we have our own oxygen. I just don't like others living too close, and their brains are smooth enough that they buy the lie and stay away."

"Do you mean to sound so selfish?" Geth asked, bothered, but giving Lars the benefit of the doubt. "Is this what you meant by not knowing how to talk right?"

"Listen," Lars said calmly, "not to be rude, but I am allowing you to be here because I am curious about you. I'm *allowing* you. But don't think for a moment that I couldn't do away with you both if I wanted."

Both Geth and Zale were so shocked by the sudden turn in Lars's personality that they almost stumbled.

"Not to be rude," Lars reiterated.

"No, that doesn't sound rude at all," Geth said sarcastically.

"I'm glad you understand," Lars replied. "Now come."

They hiked quickly across the landscape, and in no time they had reached the small hill at the center of the valley. They climbed up a long brick stairway that wound through the trees and up the hill. Zale seemed to grow stronger with each step. His breathing was labored, but his legs and body were working well.

They reached the top of the stairs, where there was a large cluster of fantastically tall trees. Their trunks were as thick as houses and their tops were so high above them that Geth and Zale couldn't see them clearly from where they stood.

"Come," Lars said. "Come."

Lars led them to a swing that hung from one of the high branches. The swing was just a piece of smooth wood with two long ropes tied to it and another rope dangling nearby.

"Take a seat," Lars told Zale.

Zale cautiously sat on the swing and held onto the ropes. He lifted his feet, resting all his weight on the swing and rocking gently.

"Normally people can easily pull themselves up," Lars said. "But your arms look like twigs."

Lars grabbed the rope that was dangling near the swing and began to pull. Easily and without any jerking motion the swing began to rise. Zale looked a bit shocked as he ascended upward into the tree branches. He held onto the ropes and hollered down.

"Where am I going?"

"You'll see," Lars said. "When you reach the platform, let the swing drop."

Zale looked up as he rose higher and higher. Lars pulled the rope effortlessly, and soon Zale was lost in the branches and no longer visible from below.

"You live in the trees?" Geth asked with a bit of jealousy.

"Among them," Lars replied. "I feel there's nothing finer to surround oneself with than trees."

"I think that's the most sensible thing you've said," Geth agreed.

Lars pulled for a little while longer and then felt the rope tug tight. He waited for a moment, then slowly let the rope feed back up through his hands. It took a few seconds, but the empty swing soon descended from above like a heavenly messenger of rope and wood. The swing dropped completely. It rocked slightly in the light wind.

"I think I'll go next," Lars said. "As much as it delights me to have two lithens in my home, I'm not sure how I feel about having two unattended lithens in my home. I'll ascend and drop the swing."

"Good," Geth said happily. "I'll finally get a few minutes alone."

"Snarky," Lars observed as he sat on the swing and took hold of the rope. "See you in the leaves."

Lars began to tug on the rope and pull himself up. The swing lifted quickly, and in a matter of seconds Geth was alone. A couple of seconds later, Clover finally spoke from the direction of Geth's left shoulder.

"Is *snarky* even a word?" Clover whispered in disgust. "I think that guy's just making things up."

"It's a word," Geth said without moving his lips. "But I definitely don't trust him."

"I don't trust your brother, either," Clover complained. "Did you hear what he said about sycophants? That's the second time he's called me a rat."

"He was just acting," Geth said, keeping his mouth still just in case Lars could still see down.

"Acting like a jerk," Clover whispered harshly. "This is all wrong. We need to get out of here. I say we leave those two up in the trees, run as fast as you can, and find our way back to Foo."

"Zale's my brother," Geth said. "I'm not leaving until this is done."

"You mean until you're dead," Clover said. "I just know that somehow you'll get killed and I'll end up one of those widow people."

"I think maybe you don't understand the word *widow*," Geth said quietly. "But we'll leave this realm as soon as Payt is finished."

"I don't think you really understand the word *finished*," Clover complained. "As soon as Payt is finished with what, dinner?"

"Until Payt is dead," Geth clarified.

"So as soon as he's dead we'll return to Foo?"

Geth nodded.

"Promise?" Clover asked hopefully and in a whisper.

"No," Geth replied. "But if fate allows."

"Fate is horrible at making and keeping promises," Clover complained. "I made a deal with fate when I was younger. It was supposed to make me taller."

"You're average height for a sycophant," Geth said.

"Right," Clover complained. "What good is average? I wanted to have at least a foot on my brothers. But did fate keep its promise?"

"I'm not sure fate's even aware it made a promise," Geth said out of the side of his mouth. "Did you keep your half?"

There was a long pause as Geth and Clover continued to stare up into the trees where the swing had disappeared.

"No," Clover finally answered. "Maybe it is my fault. I tried to keep my promise, but it's impossible to go a year without gossiping."

"Nothing's impossible," Geth said.

"It was the same year my sister left home with a sycophant magician who had been engaged to an older sycophant librarian who worked for the Council of Wonder."

"I can see why you're still the same height, then."

Geth spotted the bottom of the empty swing as it descended. It lowered until it was all the way down and Geth could easily take a seat.

"Keep invisible and close," Geth said under his breath.

"There will be nobody more see-through or more nearby," Clover assured Geth.

Geth took hold of the rope and began to pull. The swing rose almost effortlessly. There was hardly a need for any real tugging and the seat glided upward as if powered by electricity.

"This is kinda cool, I guess," Clover said, reluctant to admit that he might be enjoying anything that had to do with Lars.

Geth nodded but didn't reply verbally.

The swing went higher and higher, moving straight up through thick branches of multiple trees. The ride felt almost claustrophobic as they were surrounded by leaves of all sizes and shapes. A platform rose around them, and Geth could see Zale standing there by Lars.

Geth easily stepped onto the platform and moved the swing out from underneath him. The platform was made of wood and boxed in by leaves. Wooden planks ran from the platform to the side of a thick tree trunk and up to the most elaborate and finely finished tree house that Geth had ever seen. The house was taller than it was wide and was built up and around one of the tree trunks. Wooden beams beneath it helped to hold it up. Branches wove in and out through different bits of architecture on the home, and ivy covered the walls while thatch completed the roof.

"Come," Lars waved, heading across the path toward the house. "Come on."

Birds jumped and darted through the branches, singing songs in harmony as soft, warm sunlight filtered between the leaves and painted the scene like a serene wooded disco. For a moment things felt almost as magical and perfect as Foo.

It's sad how fleeting a moment can be.

## Chapter Seventeen

# SOMETIMES A CHAPTER HEADING IS JUST A CHAPTER HEADING

**D**oorbells are obnoxious. Whose idea was it to place a buzzer at the entrance of one's home? Anyone in their right—or wrong—mind can simply walk up to your abode and begin demanding your attention with the aid of a bell. It's the equivalent of driving up to someone who's minding their own business and laying on the horn. It's a bad approach. It's also, in my opinion, the worst possible sneak attack. Doorbells let your enemies know you're there and you're in the mood to poke things. In a perfect world, there would be no doorbells. There would be only a strand of rope that visitors would have to figure out what to do with. I suggest they practice a knot or two and then move on to bother someone else. Not that I'm opposed to people, but any real friend would simply stand on the stoop silently with a gift in hand and wait patiently for me to walk out the door.

Sadly, I guess manners are just a thing of the past.

Lars pushed open the large front door. There was no doorbell, and the door was made from polished wood with flecks of glass in it. The inside of the house was even more impressive than the outside. Beautiful pieces of handmade furniture filled the room while rugs as thick as grass blanketed the floor. A stone fireplace in the corner held a tiny fire in its belly and was keeping the room a perfect temperature. The walls were covered with art and the ceiling was painted with stars and planets. Everything looked neat and well crafted.

"Wow," Clover gasped.

Lars turned around to see who had spoken. Geth quickly opened his mouth to pretend it had been him. He coughed a couple of times and then acted speechless.

"All built by me," Lars said. "Have a seat."

Lars motioned to a red couch with cushions that looked like supportive clouds. Geth and Zale wrestled past each other to see who could sit down first.

"Ahh," Zale said as his body settled into the soft couch.

"So glad you approve," Lars said proudly. "Hungry?"

Geth and Zale looked at Lars as if they had just been asked the stupidest question ever.

"Please," Zale begged. "I'm starving."

Of course, what Zale was saying wasn't too far from the truth, seeing how he had been imprisoned and poorly fed for many years.

"Delightful," Lars said, clapping his hands. "Desperate visitors—I believe that's the very best kind."

Lars walked across the room and through a short doorway that led into a separate area.

"He's odd, right?" Zale asked in a whispered hush.

"Extremely," Geth whispered back.

"Can we be worried about it *after* we eat?" Zale asked.

Geth nodded enthusiastically.

Lars came back quickly, carrying a tray covered with food. He set the tray down on the small table in front of the couch. It was filled with sandwiches made from thick bread and dripping with meat and sauces. There were bowls filled with red berries that glistened under the low light of the comfortable room. A plate covered with mashed potatoes was surrounded by sprigs of green mint and topped with butter that scented the room in a wash of flavor.

Geth and Zale stared at the tray like two little kids looking at something grown-ups didn't want them to touch.

"Please," Lars insisted. "Dig in."

Zale became a lithen washing machine, tossing everything into his mouth and agitating it until his palate was clean. Geth tried to show some nobility, but the smell and taste of the food were intoxicating and caused both of them to act like they were under the influence of food. Every bite was a celebration and surprise that something could taste as good as it did.

"This food is amazing," Geth said honestly.

"I'm glad you approve," Lars said. "I don't have many visitors because of the condition."

Geth stopped chewing and looked Lars.

"Condition?" Geth asked with concern.

"You know," Lars said. "The one I made up about the air."

Zale didn't want to stop chewing, so he kept at it while looking upset.

"The truth is just the opposite," Lars said. "The air in this valley is incredible. In fact, it will make you live longer. But, I need to keep the riffraff away."

It was one of the hardest things Geth had done in

178

a while, but he stopped eating so as to look properly appalled.

"Don't pretend to be bothered," Lars said. "Self-preservation is a beautiful thing."

Geth suddenly felt like vomiting.

"Look at me," Lars said. "I used to live in Reality. I was a door-to-door vacuum cleaner salesman. I used to have an ex-wife, a repossessed car, and more bills than I knew what to do with. Then one day I'm sitting in a park thinking about how awful my life is and the next thing I know I'm here in Zendor. Of course, it wasn't called Zendor back then, but here I was. I popped in near the forests on the other side of the realm. I'm embarrassed to admit it, but I was scared—so scared. I thought I was sick or had gone crazy. Things were a bit different than now. Back then there were no boors, just dreams—hundreds of astronauts and cowboys and FBI agents and ballerinas all mixed together. There was no real order here, no leader, just a bunch of dreams living peacefully on the soil. I went a bit mad. I ran, and when I wasn't running, I hid. My mind was so befuddled I thought I would die from confusion. I made it across the realm and found the outside of the mountains that surround this valley."

Zale stopped eating to take a drink of some purple juice that tasted like fizzy cream.

"Your brother seems hungry," Lars observed to Geth.

The statement was too obvious to even comment on.

"I found a cave," Lars continued. "A small cave near the edge of Zendor. At first I entered it because I wanted to hide. But the cave kept going back farther and farther. Pretty soon I knew that if I went any farther I'd never be able to find my way out. Well, I was so confused I felt that it would be better to die going deeper than to live. So I kept moving farther and farther into the mountain. If there was a turn, I'd take it. If I came upon multiple tunnels, I wouldn't even pause to think. I'd just take whatever one looked bleaker. I had a candle, but it ran out. So I was stuck in the middle of the mountain in pitch-black. I figured I was dead."

"Is there more of this drink?" Zale interrupted.

Lars got up and came back with a pitcher. He filled Zale's glass and set the pitcher down next to it. Zale couldn't be bothered to thank him.

"You figured you were dead," Geth reminded Lars.

"Yes," Lars said, picking up where he had left off. "And seeing how I was going to die anyway, I thought I would just keep walking in the dark. I think I went in circles; I know I went up and down a bit; I hit my head on a low rock, all without being able to see anything. Then, I took a turn, and in the distance I could see a fleck of light. I stumbled toward it, believing it was just a messed-up hallucination from my sick brain. But the light grew bigger and brighter and I began to think I was dying and floating to the light."

"You don't look dead," Zale said between bites.

"Observant," Lars laughed. "When I stumbled into this valley, I rolled down the grass fields, drank from one of the rivers, and lay there with the sunlight covering me. I was tired, but almost instantly I began to feel stronger. There was nobody here when I arrived, but there were some scattered ruins indicating that at some point someone had lived here."

"You don't know who?" Geth asked.

"Nope," Lars said arrogantly. "And I never could think of a reason to find out. See this house we're in?" Lars asked.

Geth and Zale nodded, wondering if it were a trick question.

"I built it myself and yet I've never had a day of instruction in my life."

"I'm sure there are some flaws in it somewhere," Zale said.

"You'd think so," Lars agreed, "but I've yet to find any. That food you're eating, I not only grew it, but I prepared it. I've never had a day of food instruction in my life."

"Cooking's not that difficult," Zale scoffed.

"And people adapt to what they need to do," Geth added.

"Maybe a little," Lars said. "But the truth is that whatever you do in this valley, it comes out well. Things taste better, work goes further, and people live longer. It's not easy to die in a river that washes everyone safely to shore."

Having finally reached a point where he could no longer stuff food into his stomach, Zale stopped eating and leaned back on the couch. He breathed in as his dark eyes flickered.

"You mean *you* live longer," Zale said, as if the injustice of it all had just hit him. "You alone?"

"Of course," Lars said. "What kind of paradise would it be surrounded by the dreams of others? I never dreamed of being an astronaut or the first female president. I dreamed of being left alone and having power over others. It looks like my dreams came true."

"This is hardly power," Geth argued, his blood beginning to simmer. "The power to keep people away? The power to trick others into thinking you are something other than you are?"

"Yep," Lars said. "That's the kind of power I have.

That and the ability to destroy anyone who wishes to disagree. It beats selling vacuums."

Geth stood up.

"Sit down," Lars said amiably. "There's no need for tempers to flare. I have always wanted to know more about Foo. You and your brother are my connection. I know that this realm would not exist without Foo. I also know that, as magical as this valley was before, the restoration of your realm made it even better. I want to know more. Make me smarter; fill me in."

"No," Geth said still standing. "It's obvious that you feel no responsibility for the knowledge you hold. Why should I give you more? I can't believe these dreams in Zendor consider you wise."

"Just as I like it," Lars said. "And who's to say I'm not? Look where I am and look where they are."

"No one has ever challenged your possession of this valley?" Geth asked hotly. "Every single one of those dreams could live in peace here and no one has figured that out?"

"I can't say that nobody ever has. A few have," Lars said. "It's usually the ones that aren't the result of dreams—the humans snatched from Reality. They find out about this place and find someone who will bring them here. They barge in and think they can stay. But I dispose of them."

"So you're a killer," Zale said incredulously.

"I am the law," Lars said. "And I have killed to keep things in order. Throughout my whole life in Reality, I was beaten down by the law. Now I am at peace with it, seeing as how it benefits me personally."

"We were told you would help," Geth growled.

"I always say that," Lars smiled. "That's part of the magic. I get Stone Holders to bring me those who are strong-willed enough to want to fight, promising them that I care. Then, when they arrive, I get rid of them. If you live long enough to fight here, you will eventually meet someone who will kindly suggest you visit me. I always welcome those who come . . ."

Lars paused as if for dramatic effect.

" . . . of course, I always dispose of them as well."

Geth looked at Zale and laughed. He looked back at Lars and his blue eyes grew stormy and electric. Clouds of emotion moved over his expression, and he pushed his long hair out of his face.

"Is that a threat?" Geth asked.

"Yeah," Zale said, strength from the food and air of the valley giving him a newfound wellness. "Was that supposed to be your big dramatic moment?"

Lars looked flustered for a brief second but quickly regained control of his emotions.

"No," Lars said slimily. "I have the hardest

184

time expressing myself clearly. Forgive me if you misunderstood."

"Quite the apology," Geth said cautiously. "It's clear that you are not the man we were looking for. Now not only will I make it my responsibility to end Payt's reign of terror, but I will need to let Zendor know that the air in here won't hurt them a bit. I figure you'll have thousands of new neighbors in no time."

Lars laughed as if they were all having a fun-filled conversation.

"Could be," he smiled. "Could be."

"You need more help than I do," Zale said, creeped out by Lars. "You should see if some kid in Reality dreamt up a counselor and have him visit you. He might be able to straighten you out before you kill him."

"Come here," Lars said, jumping up. "I have something else to show you."

Lars walked out of the room and into the other area he had gone to earlier. Geth started to follow after him.

"Wait a second," Zale said, grabbing Geth by the left shoulder. "You're just going to follow him blindly?"

"My eyes are open," Geth said. "Let's see where this leads."

"I'm with your weird brother on this one," Clover

whispered to Geth from his left shoulder. "I wouldn't follow that guy anywhere. He just said he's going to kill you."

"I hope he tries," Geth said passionately. "Let's go."

"You're giving hope a bad name," Clover pointed out. He then jumped from Geth to Zale. "Just in case," Clover whispered to Zale.

Geth walked into the other room with his brother right behind him. The second room was a small kitchen with an iron stove and buckets of water in the corner. There were forks on the wooden counter and bits of food scraped together in a small pile. Against the opposite wall was a little table with only one chair. At the end of the room was a set of thin wood stairs leading up to another floor. Geth and Zale looked around but there was no sign of Lars.

"He must have gone up," Zale said.

Geth moved onto the stairs and climbed them quickly. Zale stayed right behind him, his body feeling rested and full. At the top of the thin stairs there was a spiral staircase that wrapped around the tree trunk and twisted up out of the roof and toward the top of the trees. Those stairs led up through the roof. Geth could see the crowns of other trees and a large wooden platform at the very top of the stairs. The platform was square, and the stairs met up with the bottom of it, where there was a round hole in the middle to climb through.

Geth cautiously climbed the last few stairs and stepped up onto the platform. He kept his eyes on Lars, who was standing near the far edge. Geth reached down and helped Zale come all the way up.

The two lithens stood there facing Lars, about ten feet away from him. The platform was painted white and had a wooden railing around the entire square. The railing came up about three feet high, making the whole structure look like a splintery boxing ring at the top of the world. Glancing around, Geth could see the entire valley. They were standing atop the highest point and could clearly see all the mountains that circled the valley and the hundreds of caves that looked out and over toward where they now were. It was a beautiful, frightening sight.

The entire platform swayed gently under the rocking of the soft winds. The creaking and blowing added to the overall feeling of uncertainty and surrealism. Lars stared intently at the two brothers as they stood there.

"I'm not sure that anyone but a lithen would follow me up here after I had threatened to kill them," Lars said. "Impressive."

"I'm pretty certain you're not sure of a lot of things," Geth said honestly. "It's not just lithens who have spines to stand up to fools like you."

"Well," Lars said. "You'd be hard-pressed to find any others in this realm who would do the same."

"I'm not sure who's worse for this place," Geth said. "You or Payt."

"I only harm those who bother me," Lars said. "Payt destroys everyone he can."

"You both make me sick," Geth growled.

"What a pity," Lars said. "We were getting along so well at the start."

"You mean back when you were pretending to be human?" Geth asked.

"Such bite," Lars snipped. "I have to kill you two. I mean, I have no choice. You understand that, don't you?"

"We're pretty clear on the fact that you are un-stable," Zale said. "That and the fact that you love to hear yourself talk."

"It's a shame you don't understand," Lars scoffed. "There's no stopping Payt. I simply am smart enough to understand that. I have found a way to live comfortably despite him."

Geth shivered.

"Oh, that's right," Lars said, smiling and waving

his hands as if it were a friendly conversation. "You lithens see no value in comfort. I must say, I'm not terribly impressed by your breed. Your brother is useless, and you, Geth, are too passionate for justice to ever succeed. Don't you know that the truly wise understand and accept that some must suffer so that others can enjoy?"

Geth's simmering blood began to fully boil. He hated Lars. And whereas it was pretty uncommon for a lithen to hate, it was even more uncommon for a lithen like Geth to hate as heavily as he now did.

His blue eyes sizzled, competing with the sun for rays of heat.

"You see all those hundreds of tunnels," Lars said, motioning with his hands to the caves in the far-off mountains. "Almost all of those have telescopes that are looking down at this platform. Look."

Even from a great distance away, it was clear to see that all the many tunnels had tiny figures gathered at the mouths of them.

"This is where I signal others," Lars said. "This is where I instruct and lead. This is where I trick the realm of Zendor to believe in me as a mythical figure. There's not much entertainment for Stone Holders as they hide. They're a captive audience that lives off my whims. In a moment they will see you lunge at me.

They will then see me defend myself and witness once again that even a lithen cannot destroy me. Correction: even two lithens can't destroy me. My legendary status will only climb. This is a very good day for me."

"Do I ever sound that crazy?" Zale asked with concern.

"A little," Geth said honestly. "Only when you talk about doing nothing for the rest of your life."

"Well, look what doing something has gotten us," Zale argued.

"You two," Lars said with a smile. "Stop fighting one another and attack me."

Geth's insides were threatening to jump out of his outsides. His inner Ezra rose up into his throat like bad soup after a heavy meal. Clover was invisible and now sitting on Geth's right shoulder. Like a tiny, hairy angel he whispered into Geth's ear.

"It's not worth it," Clover said softly so that only Geth could hear. "Let's get away from this nutcase."

Geth took another deep breath.

"It's not worth it," Clover whispered again.

Geth looked out at all the tunnels and caves in the distance. "We're not going to attack you, Lars," he said calmly. "We can accomplish what we need without your death. Come on, Zale."

Geth motioned for his brother to follow him back down the stairs.

"Good for you," Lars laughed. "But before you go, I want to tell you something I'm reminded of. This is just like the time a man from New York was snatched into Zendor. After he heard about me, he found me, thinking I would help him save the realm. I invited him up here to see how beautiful things were and then forcefully expressed to him how much I could never let him live. He too did the valiant thing. He climbed back down those stairs, only to die half an hour later from the poison I had earlier put in his food."

"You poisoned our food?" Geth asked happily, his insides growing excited by the fact that he might still get the chance to set Lars straight.

"The way the boors tell that story is that the man died because of the air."

"You're mad," Geth growled. "You've poisoned us."

"I'm not stupid," Lars said.

"I changed my mind," Clover whispered, switching shoulders and acting more like a little devil now. "I think you should hurt him."

"He didn't poison us," Zale argued. "He's bluffing."

"Can you be sure?" Lars asked.

"Get ready," Clover whispered to Geth.

Geth looked confused and wondered what Clover meant. Clover, on the other hand, was quickly moving into position. He jumped from off of Geth and quietly hopped back behind Lars. He climbed up on the wooden rails and with one swift leap he sprang out and, as kindly as he could, jabbed his claws into Lars's derriere. Lars screamed and leapt forward, directly toward Geth. Geth spun and kicked Lars in the chest with the bottom of his right foot. Lars flew back, crashing into the same spot on the rails where Clover had been. The hit looked horrific, but Lars jumped up immediately.

Geth charged at him.

Geth wrapped his arms around Lars's waist, twisted him back, and threw him onto the platform with such force there was a pop. The noise echoed through the valley like a single clap of applause. Geth rolled off of Lars as Zale backed away from the action.

Lars sprang right up onto his feet once more. Aside from the blood where Clover had pierced him, he looked no worse for wear.

"Dirty play," Lars said. "You have an invisible helper. Of course, if I know anything about the curiosity of sycophants, I know that yours probably snuck at least one bite of that food. And with his small body, the effect will work even quicker."

"Well, then, I'd better strike fast," an invisible Clover yelled, slicing his claws down Lars's back.

The cuts caused Lars's knees to buckle and send his body forward. Once again it looked like Lars was attacking Geth. Geth grabbed Lars by the ears and threw him to the ground. He then put his foot on his back to keep him pinned down. Lars bucked and threw Geth's leg up into the air while hopping back onto his own feet.

"You can't keep me down," Lars bragged. "I'm too powerful. This air has made me super strong. And everyone watching will witness my greatness grow in leaps and bounds as I finish you. Come on, Geth, be a man—attack me."

Clover hopped back up onto the rails behind Lars. He jumped as hard as he could and slammed his feet into the back of Lars's head. Lars stumbled forward and Geth used the motion to attack. A thin blade of metal slipped out from Lars's wrist as he produced a hidden knife. He aimed for Geth's chest, but Geth was too quick. The knife nicked Geth's left shoulder as he moved to the side and twisted around.

Geth had a surprise of his own.

Geth produced a fork he had taken from Lars's

kitchen and shoved it into Lars's right side. The super-strong vacuum salesman from New York went down. He crumbled to the ground in a heap of heartless human.

Geth bent over, grabbing his own shoulder and trying to catch his breath. Zale moved to his side.

"Thanks for the help," Geth said sarcastically, breathing hard.

"Sorry," Zale apologized. "I used to fight."

"Well, we need you to fight again," Geth said angrily. "Things must change. Clover!" Geth called.

"Right here, toothpick," Clover said, appearing on Geth's right shoulder.

"We're so lucky you're on our side," Geth complimented him. "Smart moves."

"I'm happy for any chance to use my claws," Clover said, waving off the admiration. "And I'd hate to sound all braggy like Lars, but I do come in handy."

"Geth!" Zale yelled.

Lars was back on his feet and lunging toward Geth from behind. Zale charged into Lars, and with one huge movement he pushed him across the platform. Lars slammed into the rail, and Zale pushed him harder, sending the selfish hermit over the edge and hundreds of feet down to the bottom of the hill below him.

Zale fell to his knees and looked down over the edge of the platform. Geth and Clover moved in and gazed down with him.

"Wow," Clover said reverently. "Why didn't he fly? I thought he was supposed to be all super strong."

"Being super strong doesn't make you fly," Geth said solemnly. "Nobody could survive that."

"I don't know what came over me," Zale whispered. "I just reacted."

"You probably saved my life," Geth admitted.

"Hey, do you guys remember how I helped Geth earlier?" Clover asked, bothered that the conversation wasn't revolving around him anymore. "I helped him at least a couple of times."

"You were pretty amazing," Geth praised him.

"Not that any of this really matters," Zale said sadly. "If we were poisoned, things are about to grow pretty dark."

"Don't worry about that," Clover said. "I just may have been in the kitchen when Lars was pouring that stuff on the food. It wasn't poison."

"Are you sure?" Geth asked hopefully.

"Yeah," Clover insisted. "He had two little bottles. The one he poured on the food was piñon."

"Piñon?" Geth asked, confused.

"I'm sure of it," Clover promised. "The other bottle was artichoke juice. Look, I saved the bottle."

Clover fished out a small glass bottle from his void and read it aloud.

"Piñon."

Geth took the bottle from Clover and read it himself.

"Poison," Geth said with concern.

"Is that how you pronounce that?" Clover asked. "I thought the *s* was silent."

"Do you have that other bottle?" Zale asked frantically.

"No," Clover said. "I thought that would be stealing . . . okay, I might have it."

"Here," Geth said sticking his hand out. "Where is it?"

Clover rooted around in his void and pulled out a little bottle filled with a dark liquid. It had a small label on the front that read:

"Antidote," Geth cheered.

"You need to learn how to read," Zale said sternly to Clover.

Geth handed the bottle to Zale, who took a quick drink. Clover took a smaller sip, and Geth had the rest.

"I don't like the taste," Clover complained while smacking his lips.

"It tastes better than dying."

"Of course," Clover agreed. "But it just seems like any real antidote should be mint flavored. I mean, if you're going to live, you might as well have nice breath."

Geth patted Clover on the head. "You saved us again."

"Make sure you tell Lilly."

"There's no way I won't," Geth promised.

All three of them stood up and walked over to the stairs. The tops of the trees swayed just as they had before. Birds and warmth filled the air as if a life hadn't just been lost. Being lithens, Geth and Zale knew the role that death played, but it was never comfortable harming another, even when the evil was obvious. They all took one final look and started down the stairs. Despite the fact that they were stuck in Zendor and there was still the problem of Payt, things seemed peaceful. Clover cleared his throat.

"So who do you think gets Lars's house?" Clover asked.

Geth gave Clover a look strong enough to let him know that now was not the time to ask those kinds of things.

"Right," Clover said. "It's just that I know he doesn't have any relatives here, and judging by how he acted, I'm guessing he didn't have a lot of friends."

"Clover," Geth said.

"Right," Clover said again. "I know I sort of saved all of our lives and all, but I'll just ask later."

Geth and Zale climbed down the stairs while Clover sat on top of Geth's head trying to act respectful.

"What now?" Zale asked.

"Now?" Geth said. "Well, I'd say things just got a little worse for Payt."

"That makes no sense," Zale insisted.

"When he gets like this it usually means things are about to get interesting," Clover explained. "It's always dumbest before the dawn."

"I think you're quoting that wrong," Geth said as they reached the bottom of the spiral stairs and descended the thin stairs into the kitchen. "But I think I have an idea and a use for this valley."

"You know, Lilly would love this kitchen," Clover cooed.

"You're not getting his house," Geth reiterated.

Clover frowned and disappeared.

## Chapter Eighteen

# TAKE A LONG, DEEP BREATH

Some words are better than others. I like the word *pavement* better than *asphalt*. I just do. *Sofa* over *plaza, chump* is better than *dump,* and I'm a big fan of the word *ambisinister* while I have nothing but hard feelings for the word *shunt.* There is a social order in the world of words. Big words look down on little words, medium words have a difficult time with hyphenated words, and staple words like *the* and *and* would be nothing but *th* and *nd* without the help of some vowels. I met a woman who calls underwear *breezies,* and I know a man who calls soda *pop.* I think that one's particularly sad—I mean, it's like calling juice *mom.* Then there are the fancy speakers with their special words. They're the kind of people who call teenagers *ruffians* and rears ends *derrieres*. Those kinds of people probably should be tagged and followed.

Words are like printed T-shirts: Some are fun to read, and some are just a waste of letters.

Geth, Zale, and Clover found Lars's body on the hill below the tree house and buried him. Geth said a few words, and Clover tried to make himself cry. He couldn't do it, so he pulled a bit of tear gas gum from his void and chewed. The mist from his mouth caused not only Clover but Geth and Zale to weep uncontrollably. Like most good sycophants, Clover carried plenty of tissue to help, but even he didn't have enough to help now. By the time they had reached the edge of the valley, their eyes were red and incredibly swollen.

"You're cleaning out that void," Geth insisted.

"That's the hardest I've cried in my life," Zale sniffed.

They hiked up to the same tunnel they had previously occupied. They could see Nick up on the stone balcony waiting there. Behind Nick were dozens of other Stone Holders. Geth looked around at some of the other tunnels close by. The entrance of every tunnel he could see was filled with Stone Holders looking out at them with quiet uncertainty.

"This kind of thing never happened in my cell," Zale mumbled.

"You can thank me later," Geth said facetiously.

Geth leapt up onto the bottom of the balcony and began pulling himself up. Nick reached over and helped yank him up. The two of them then assisted Zale in his climb over. Once they were both on the balcony, Geth and Zale stood up and faced the crowd. All eyes of all the Stone Holders rested uncomfortably on them. There was still no sound from any of them.

"Lars is dead," Geth said straightforwardly.

There was no reaction from the crowd. Geth hoped there had been plenty of witnesses who had seen through the telescopes what had transpired.

"It wasn't our plan," Geth informed them.

"We saw the fight," Nick said. "It was hard to tell who struck first."

"We had no desire to kill him," Geth told them. "He gave us no choice."

"I believe you," Nick said, holding his cowboy hat in his hand. "We all saw you bury him. That was real kind of you. You were mighty overcome with grief. I never seen anyone weep like that."

"That wasn't . . ." Zale started to say.

Geth elbowed Zale in the ribs to shut him up.

"Only people with kind hearts could be so moved," Nick said.

Geth and Zale remained quiet.

"It's a shame," Nick said. "Lars was a very wise man."

"Are you sure of that?" Zale asked.

"He always said he was wise," a Stone Holder behind Nick informed them.

"Such a pity," Nick said. "This beautiful valley with no one to live in it."

"Um," Geth said with a small laugh. "There's nothing dangerous about the air in this valley. Lars was misinformed."

"That's not true," an athletic Stone Holder hollered from another tunnel. "Some have tried and not lived through the night."

"That's because that nitwit Lars killed them," Zale shouted, no longer able to defend the selfish Lars.

The crowd reacted now. Everyone gasped, and some began to yell and stomp their feet. Geth held up his hands.

"Listen," Geth hollered. "It's true that we had no desire to kill Lars, but it's also true that he wasn't a good man. He's kept this from so many. The air in the valley is no different from the air in the caves."

"I don't believe you," a Stone Holder in a business suit yelled. "Lars said so himself."

"Lars cared only for himself," Geth shouted. "He had no desire to share this."

"Well, I'm not taking a chance," a Stone Holder in a football helmet barked. "I don't believe it."

"I believe it," Nick said, surprising everyone. "You're a lithen, and there ain't no way a liar would cry like you did at the death of another. Besides, I never really believed there was danger. I've stood on this balcony for hours and days and never had no sickness or death."

"Lars was no different from you," Geth said. "And he lived just fine. This valley is a safe home to all of the inhabitants of Zendor."

Nick smiled. "I always did want to walk through those grassy fields. I'm so sick of caves and darkness."

Nick jumped over the balcony like he was hopping onto a horse. He landed on the grass and rolled a few feet.

The crowds gasped and mumbled.

Nick stood up. His legs shook a bit as he took in a big breath of air. He exhaled and looked back at the mountains.

"I ain't dead," he yelled.

The crowd began to jabber and argue with each

other. Geth could see a couple of Stone Holders from other tunnels drop down and begin running into the valley. Nick had turned and was running farther into the valley. He reached one of the streams and knelt down to take a drink of water. He stood back up and yelled as loud as he could.

"Still not dead, and the water tastes sweet!"

Stone Holders were not known for being great free thinkers. They were dreams that had come to life and been forced to live in caves and only come out at night. They were too frightened to fight and too disorganized to be effective in any way. It was no surprise that Payt's voice could turn their minds to mush and control them because they weren't deep thinkers to begin with. These Stone Holders here had lived for years and never really questioned why they couldn't breathe the air in the valley. Now as one of theirs simply tasted the water and lived to tell about it, they were all converted. Sure, Geth could have been tricking them and leading them into one massive slaughter, but luckily for them that wasn't the case.

Stone Holders dripped and tumbled from the caves all around the valley, running through the grass and trees like children. Geth and Zale watched them all streaming out of the tunnels in excitement.

Clover materialized on Geth's right shoulder.

"Great," Clover complained. "There goes the neighborhood. I can only imagine what they'll do to my house . . . that house," Clover corrected.

"We need to get back out of here," Geth said. "I've got to find Jill. She can bring her people in here."

"Can't we just head home?" Clover begged. "Look at all these people who now have a place to live. And they all lived happily ever after," Clover said dramatically.

"No," Geth insisted. "There's someone I still need to deal with."

"I bet it's a girl," Clover moaned.

"Payt," Geth reminded him.

"Wait," Clover said confused. "Payt's not a girl. He's just in that fairy troupe. By the way, didn't he say he was thirteenth division last time, and now he's fourteenth? I think he's promoting himself."

"I'm with Clover," Zale said as the noise of Stone Holders rejoicing became almost unbearable. "You should get out of this realm while you can."

"We're not getting out," Geth said. "And when we do, you're coming with us."

"No," Zale insisted.

"Don't argue with him," Clover complained. "He never backs down."

"I'm not arguing," Zale insisted. "This feels nice.

Hurray for the Stone Holders. Now they can hide in comfort. But the truth is, Payt still rules, and these people are merely trapped in a different spot. There's no real escape from Payt and no exit to Zendor."

"Eve escaped," Geth reminded his brother. "She brought us here."

"Eve escaped?" Zale spat. "Where is she now? Oh, that's right, she's under the influence of Payt's voice and being forced to do his will. I bet she's happy about her escape."

"We'll change that," Geth argued. "This is a beginning, not an end."

Geth headed back down the tunnel with Zale following. They passed Stone Holders who had heard the news and were heading toward the light.

"Do you remember how to get out?" Clover asked.

"I think so," Geth replied. "There weren't too many turns."

Geth navigated them down and through the tunnels perfectly, despite the fact that Clover kept insisting they were going the wrong way.

"It'll be light outside," Clover reminded Geth. "What if there are boors?"

"I don't mind waiting a few more hours to change a thousand lives."

"Nice," Clover said. "That line's definitely going in the biography."

Geth smiled and continued to lead.

"I bet Edgar has really missed me," Clover added.

"I bet you're right," Geth agreed.

Nighttime couldn't come soon enough.

## Chapter Nineteen

# BOXED IN, CLOSED UP, PUSHED OUT

It has been said by more than one smart-looking person in a lab coat and glasses that questions can lead to answers. Of course, a few smart people wearing ties and polished shoes have also said that questions can also lead to more questions. I suppose that's true. I once asked a man why he felt it was necessary to harm me. He then questioned my authority to ask such a question. His attitude caused me to question his approach, and we both ended up confused and questioning our place in a world where questions were so freely thrown about. He believed that we were here to form questions. I felt we were here to find answers.

There's no question I'm right.

Geth had a lot of questions. In Foo, he had grown

208

up a member of an elite pedigree. As a lithen, he had always been respected by most and hated by some. He had known happiness and sorrow, but embraced them both in ways that only a lithen could. Now, as he sat in a large cavern in the center of Zendor, he had more questions about who he was and if he was doing the right thing than he had ever had before. It was as if the lithen in him was being drained and real concern and emotions were visiting him for the very first time.

"Are you okay?" Clover asked. "You're so quiet."

"I hope we're in the right spot," Geth said, surprised to hear the words coming out of his mouth.

"Whoa," Clover said reverently. "I don't think I've ever heard you say that."

"Foo seems so far away," Geth added softly.

"Finally," Clover cheered with enthusiasm. "This is what I've been saying. Let's ditch this plan and find our way out. But we've gotta bring Edgar."

Edgar was currently asleep on the cave floor. He had waited patiently for them while they had visited Lars, and had been by Clover's side ever since they had come out. Geth looked at Edgar and smiled.

"We should just have him take apart Payt," Clover suggested.

"I wish we could," Geth said. "But Payt's voice would stop him."

"Fine," Clover said assertively. "Then let's get out of here and return to Foo."

"Really?" Geth asked. "You could bail on everyone here in Zendor—all those who are now lined up to help finish this?"

"They have the plan," Clover said. "They don't need us. We can find a substitute. It might be good for them to do it on their own."

"The plan was my idea," Geth reminded him.

"And it's an okay plan," Clover said skeptically. "I just have a hard time getting behind something that's dependent on me being a part."

"That's probably a smart way for you to live," Geth joked.

It had been over a week since Lars had died, and Zendor was already changing. The Stone Holders and Those Who Hide had gotten word of the safety the valley provided, and a secret and powerful exodus had begun. As Payt burned fields and destroyed any structure he could find in an attempt to locate Geth, those who had once only hidden and lived in the dark were making their way across Zendor to hide safely in the valley.

"We can get out," Clover said happily. "We've done our part. That valley is filling with more and more beings every hour. Think how many people are safe because of . . . because of . . ."

"Because of you?" Geth asked with a smile.

"I didn't want to brag," Clover said humbly.

"So what were you saying to all those women the other night?" Geth asked. "That wasn't bragging?"

"I was just filling them in," Clover insisted. "What I did or didn't do is history and I want to make sure they record it properly."

Geth patted Clover on the head.

"It's a dangerous plan," Geth said with excitement and worry. "Are you sure you want in?"

"No," Clover said passionately. "I want out. Out of here and back to Foo. Lilly has to be sick about me by now."

"Yeah," Geth said solemnly. "I wish I could at least let Phoebe know I'm okay."

"You're not okay," Clover reminded him. "You're acting weird. Ever since that Lars guy bit it, I mean perished, you seem sort of sad. I didn't think lithens could be sad."

"I didn't either," Geth said, still not understanding what was happening himself.

"The plan could go wrong," Clover reminded Geth.

"But if it goes right, I'll get a chance to talk to Payt face-to-face," Geth said seriously.

"Most people wouldn't see that as a perk."

"He has to be stopped."

"What happens if things go nuts?" Clover asked. "Payt has a lot of boors. So many of the people we once knew are now fighting against us."

"Well, let's quit, then," Geth suggested.

"I hate it when you raise my hopes like that," Clover complained. "And what about your brother?"

"Zale's committed," Geth said. "The air from that valley has made him a new person. He's helped build the wagons and right now is out in the field getting things ready. I hardly recognize him."

Geth was right about Zale. Since Lars had perished, Zale had stepped up and fully embraced Geth's plan to fight. He had also spent time helping those who were traveling the caves and moving to the valley. He was a changed lithen. The transformation gave Geth hope but also brought up strong feelings of sadness over the absence of all the others he cared for.

"Tell me again how this plan is going to work?" Clover asked Geth.

"Okay," Geth said. "We've built three wooden wagons similar to the one we've seen Payt driving. Except there's a major difference."

"The secret compartment at the bottom," Clover whispered excitedly.

"Right," Geth said. "Each compartment can fit one person. Zale, Nick, and I will hide in the three wagons. The wagons will be pushed onto the main road, where Jill and others will pretend to drive them in broad daylight. When the boors give chase, Jill and the others will abandon the wagons. The boors will then do what they always do when they find any person or thing out of place. They'll take the wagons to Pencilbottom Castle."

"Just like when that one guy built that tower," Clover chimed in. "And Zale said they took the whole thing to the castle?"

"Yes," Geth answered. "And Zale is certain that the wagons will be put in the large compound near the castle. That's where all the objects and oddities the boors bring in are placed. It's perfect because we will be safely in the castle grounds without anyone knowing."

"I'd be impressed, but remember, that's where we once had to escape from."

"I know," Geth said with excitement. "But now we're sneaking in. Then when night falls we'll slip out of the wagons and take care of Payt."

"This is just like that one story," Clover said in

a hushed voice, "where that guy builds that wooden animal and hides inside of it."

"Trojan horse," Geth said.

"No," Clover insisted. "The guy's name was Gregg, and I think the story was called 'Wooden Surprise.'"

"Right," Geth said skeptically. "This is just like 'Wooden Surprise.'"

"Also, you left two things out," Clover said.

"What?"

"One, I'll be hiding in your wagon with you."

Geth nodded. "True—that's a great strength to our plan."

"And two," Clover listed, "there are about a hundred things that can go wrong."

"But we just need a couple of things to go right," Geth said positively.

"Pencilbottom Castle is filled with traps," Clover reminded him. "If you remember correctly, you and I were both caught in one."

"Zale has given us great information about the safest ways to move around the castle," Geth said. "He spent many years there in that cell, and he's heard and learned a few things over the years. We'll still have to be careful, but we'll have the upper hand. We know where Payt will be, and we know how to get there."

"I think I'm going to throw up thinking about it," Clover admitted.

"Then don't think," Geth instructed. "Besides, it's time to move."

Clover hopped over and patted Edgar on the head. The big beast didn't even stir.

"Hopefully when he wakes up we'll almost be back," Clover said. "I'll be honest, though, it scares me to leave him."

"Do what you fear most," Geth said wisely, "and the death of fear is certain."

"I have a hard time killing spiders," Clover complained. "Not to mention fear."

Geth picked up Clover and put him on his right shoulder. He then walked down the long tunnel and out into the field of crops where the wagons had been built and hidden. There were a number of women gathered around the wagons waiting to help push. Jill was there, still wearing a sweater around her neck and bossing people around. Zale and Nick were already in their wagons preparing to crawl into the hidden compartments. Zale looked stronger, and there was life in his eyes now. His dark beard had been shaved off, and the resemblance to Geth was much more visible.

"This is foolish," Zale said supportively to his brother.

"I know," Geth replied.

"We'll be fine," Nick said. "I know there's danger ahead, but I kinda like the feeling of excitement on the back of my neck."

"You sound more like a lithen than Zale and I do," Geth joked.

"Thank you kindly," Nick replied. He then took off his cowboy hat and with ceremony tossed it out into the group of women. A girl in a bathing suit and cap caught the hat and cheered.

"Remember," Geth said, "we wait one hour after dark. Then open the compartment and follow your route. The first one to finish Payt wins."

Nick and Zale clapped.

Jill helped Geth and Clover up into their wagon. A woman dressed in a pink skirt with pink leather shoes, like Eve and Anna, moved the large wooden plank to show Geth the compartment.

"You're very brave," she said breathlessly as Geth started to climb in.

"Thank you," Clover replied.

Geth lay down in the bottom of the compartment with Clover.

"I wish I was going with you," the woman in pink said, blushing.

"Mindy," Jill chastised. "Stop harassing Geth."

Jill stepped over and helped Mindy slide the large, heavy board into place.

"Thanks," Geth called from inside the compartment.

"Anytime," Jill cooed.

It was dark inside the small compartment, but a tiny crack directly above Geth's eyes allowed him to see out just a bit and kept the space from being pitch-black. Geth's legs were stretched straight out and he was laying his head on a soft piece of cloth. Geth bent his arms and closed two hooks that held the plank in place on top of him. Clover bunched himself up on the right side of Geth's head.

"I hate small spaces," Clover whispered.

"They're not my favorite either," Geth agreed.

"You know, this is way more dangerous for you," Clover said quietly. "If we get caught, I can always go invisible."

"I know," Geth said. "If something goes wrong, you have to find a way back to Foo alone."

"I would never leave you," Clover said. "I mean, I love Leven and Winter and I really love Lilly, but I couldn't leave."

The sound of Jill settling onto the front seat of the wagon and other dreams gathering behind could be heard. Geth looked up through the sliver of a crack and could see the back of Jill's hair as she sat.

"This is it," Geth whispered.

The women began to push the wagons through the fields toward the large road that cut through Zendor. Their wagon rolled quickly, and Geth and Clover banged against the boards as it bounced. In less than half an hour they had reached the main road.

The wagons were shoved out of the fields and onto the dirt road. The women then continued to push the wagons, heading in the direction of the castle. Jill pretended to drive her wagon while she was pushed.

"This had better work," Clover said nervously. "Don't you think the boors will notice the wagons are being pushed and think something's up?"

"I'm hoping they're too dumb," Geth said. "Their only orders are to bring back what they overtake. I don't think they'll even realize that these wagons have no horses."

In less than ten minutes Geth and Clover heard screaming outside the wagon. Geth could see Jill dash away from the seat she had been sitting in.

"No more talking," Geth urged.

"I'll be perfectly quiet," Clover promised. "Starting . . . now!"

The wagon they were in slowed and came to a stop

as the women all ran from the scene and into fields to hide. The boors smothered the wagons, looking for any life. Geth could see them stepping on the board over them and searching the wagon for supplies. When they found nothing, they did the only thing their confused brains knew how to do. They followed the order they had been given and began to push the wagons to Pencilbottom Castle.

"I think it's working," Clover said.

Geth held his finger to his lips.

The three wagons moved on, heading toward the castle and mimicking the lesser known story from history, "Wooden Surprise."

## Chapter Twenty

# DARKNESS
# ASCENDS

I don't feel good about space. Sure I like outer space, but plain, common, nothing-happening space makes me uncomfortable. I get uneasy when I see blank pages full of space. Any empty space between two books on a bookshelf makes me sad. Tetris is a fine game until you end up with some open space you can't fill. But perhaps the worst kind of space is the space between two people when they're apart. Sure, it's nice to have a good deal of space between you and that weird grocer who always stares at you. But it is horrible to have too much wide-open space between you and someone you love.

No space is lonelier, larger, or more of a vacuum.

Geth's emotions were no longer his own. He

felt the vastness of the space between him and those he loved. Being a lithen had always been a badge of honor, but at the moment he worried that it might be the problem that would ultimately create a kind of space between him and those he loved forever. There was almost no space between him and Clover as they lay hidden in the false compartment at the bottom of the wagon. But it wasn't Clover that Geth was thinking of.

It was Phoebe.

The longing that Geth had left behind in Foo was weighing heavily on his heart and mind. He had loved her before he was taken to Zendor, but as his insides and emotions morphed and changed, he found himself aching for her in ways that were new and frightening. Now, as he lay in the dark, the heavy possibility that he might never see her again made him doubt almost everything he had ever known.

The boors had done just as Geth had hoped. They had brought the wagons through the gate, pushed them through the abandoned town of Finis, and deposited them behind Pencilbottom Castle next to other wagons and contraptions that had been brought in or created by Payt. The boors had then departed, and not a single sound other than birds and wind had been heard since.

It took everything Clover had in him to keep quiet. The compartment was warm, and the cramped quarters were giving Clover nervous legs and making his brain anxious. Clover tried to speak a couple of times, but Geth kept putting his hand over his mouth.

After many hours they could see through the thin crack that the purple sky was finally turning black.

"There's no one out there," Clover said under his breath. "It's been silent since we got here. Plus, now that it's dark, any boors will be frozen."

"Still," Geth insisted in a hushed voice, "it's best to stay quiet."

"Do you think Zale's and Nick's wagons are next to ours?" Clover asked.

"I have no way of knowing for sure," Geth whispered. "But I would think so."

"How will we know when it's been an hour?" Clover asked in the lowest volume possible.

"You always say that you can feel if Lilly's still alive," Geth reminded him. "Just see if you can feel what time it is for her and tell me when it's been an hour."

"Okay," Clover said happily, glad to have an assignment that involved thinking of Lilly.

The sky they could see through the thin crack became completely black; the night was out in full force.

" . . . twenty-seven, twenty-eight. Wait," Clover whispered. "How many seconds are in an hour?"

"Three thousand, six hundred," Geth answered.

"No, not in a day," Clover said. "An hour?"

"Three thousand, six hundred," Geth repeated.

"Fine," Clover complained. "I'll figure it out myself."

Geth could hear the sound of bats flying overhead and leaves blowing lightly in the trees to the north. The sounds were those of comfort and familiarity, but Geth's heart beat like neither of those things were in play. Geth could feel the strength and confusion building in his soul. He wanted only to get out and finish Payt. He could see nothing else. No other solution. No answer that did not involve him destroying Payt so he could go home. Geth had wondered numerous times if he was forcing fate, but he didn't care any longer. Payt's death was the only solution he could see. The thought made him sick and a bit mad in the head.

"You were right," Clover whispered. "I was dividing instead of subtracting. Math is just such a—"

Lights went on somewhere near the wagon. Through the crack, Geth could tell that there were two different light sources near each of the wagon's front corners. The light flickered and moved, indicating that it was being produced by flames.

Both Geth's and Clover's hearts began to beat like kettledrums being played by a dozen people. Clover put his hand to his heart to try to quiet it a bit.

The wagon creaked and shook as someone climbed up on it. Geth could see two figures moving about. The movement was followed by the sound of something being hammered directly above them.

"Are they trying to bust us out?" Clover whispered nervously.

"No," Geth said, suddenly realizing what was happening. "They're trying to keep us in. They know we're here."

"I wasn't that loud," Clover said defensively.

Geth started to kick and push at the latches that he had closed. The latches popped, but the board would not slide open. There was more hammering above. Clover kicked at the lid and scurried around the space, pushing every inch. Geth shifted his arms and pushed with all of his might. His muscles strained and his body screamed as he fought to break out.

His arms collapsed and he stopped pushing. He took in a few deep breaths in preparation to push again. More torches were lit, and the space that Geth could see through the slit became brighter. He could see the backs of two boors as they nailed shut what might end up as his coffin.

"Stop," Geth commanded. "Stop!"

The wagon rocked as someone new climbed up on it.

"Oh, they won't listen to you," Payt said, kneeling down and looking into the tiny crack at Geth. The red scratch marks Geth could see looked infected. "They have the worst manners. They refuse to listen to anyone else but me."

"Payt," Geth seethed.

Through the slit, Payt could see only a tiny line of Geth's blue eyes. But the small line was all Geth needed to show off a huge amount of anger.

"My," Payt said. "I would think you liked it in there. After all, it wasn't me that put you in. You must have done that all by yourself."

"Open this up," Geth ordered.

"I wouldn't do that," a third voice said. "He's got that rat in there. You open it once and you'll have him to contend with."

Zale's face slipped into view above the crack.

Clover's gasp bounced around the small compartment. All the anger and uncertainty that had been building in Geth died in an instant. His arms and legs and head seemed to pop and then deflate painfully under the realization of what was happening and who had betrayed him.

"I don't believe it," Geth said sadly.

Payt and Zale both leaned in so that all Geth could see were their two awful faces.

"What are you doing?" Geth asked in disbelief. "Where's Nick?"

"He didn't make it," Zale said. "There was an accident."

"This makes no sense," Geth said kicking at the wall of his box.

"It's pretty simple, actually," Zale said. "My intention was always to get back. The moment our wagons were brought beyond the gate, I slipped out and pledged my allegiance. I know there's no way out of this realm, and I know there's no one with any real power besides Payt. So the act of betraying others to get something in return just came naturally."

"Naturally?" Geth snapped.

"Don't sound all righteous," Zale insisted. "I told you to leave me. I got you out and set you free, but you refused to let me be."

"Of course, all's well that ends well," Payt said. "For years I've been offering your brother a chance to join the ranks. But he refused. He just sat in that cell preferring ease over effort."

"It requires so much less," Zale said casually.

"But with you taking him out and forcing him to

fight, he has seen the light," Payt said. "To be more specific, he has seen the scorch stone. Discovered what I've been looking for for years. What a lucky find. What's that called, Zale?"

"Fate," Zale said in a sinister voice.

"Of course," Payt smiled. "Fate. Now we can light those tunnels and caves bright enough to allow my boors to destroy things underground. Zale has also memorized the paths and knows just how we should tackle the task of destroying all Those Who Hide in the valley. The same valley I could never have gotten to without your help. They'll be sitting ducks. Nobody will avoid my voice, and in the end the whole of Zendor will be mine."

"Zale," Geth pleaded. "You can't want this."

"What I want is luxury," Zale said. "Luxury and quiet. Payt has promised me both."

"The finest room," Payt agreed. "The most attentive servants and any comfort he seeks. It's the least I can do. Loyalty should be rewarded."

"Luxury?" Geth spat. "In the end your loyalty brings you luxury?"

"Nobody lives forever, Geth," Zale said urgently. "I prefer to live my days in comfort and with some meat on my bones."

"We're brothers," Geth tried.

"I suppose in blood," Zale mocked. "But you left me here too many years. It's not my fault I forgot where I came from."

"I think I'm going to be sick," Geth moaned.

"I think you're going to be dead," Payt corrected him.

"Please," Geth reasoned, the fight draining from his being. "Let us out. There are other ways."

"That's true," Payt said snobbishly. "But here's the way I see it. I'm building a new wall. So many boors these days—labor is dirt cheap and I'm in the mood to build things higher and wider. I've decided to give you the privilege of being a tiny part of what I'm creating. We've placed the wagon with you inside it right here on purpose. Now we just cover you with concrete and fill the forms built around you, and you will be a permanent part of the structure. Someday, when the world of Zendor looks back on the wealth and power I've amassed, I will be able to look at that section of wall and realize that even a lithen couldn't stop me."

"I told you it was foolish to fight," Zale said. "I told you Payt would win."

"Some people just won't heed a warning," Payt said, smiling wickedly.

"Zale," Geth implored, "we're brothers."

"It's just death," Zale said defensively. "Remember what you said: 'Everybody dies.'"

Payt and Zale stood up and climbed off the wagon.

"Begin," Payt ordered someone.

Geth and Clover couldn't see everything that was happening, but through the slit they could see a large metal chute swing over their wagon. Someone yelled something and a low rumbling sound began.

"This isn't good," Geth said.

"Wait," Clover complained. "That's my line."

Wet concrete began to drop from the chute and cover the wagon. Big wads of the heavy mixture plopped down forcefully.

Geth felt as if everything he had ever believed was being tested in the extreme. The hope he had professed to live by suddenly seemed like a fable or a cruel joke.

A fistful of concrete landed on the open slit and completely blocked the little bit of light Geth and Clover did have.

"What do you know," Clover said quietly. "Darkness does ascend."

Geth was lost in thought.

"Hey," Clover said, nudging Geth's left shoulder. "I know I always say you talk too much, but you're welcome to say something comforting now.

You should know, also, that you're nothing like your brother. There has never been a lithen like you."

"Thanks, Clover," Geth said solemnly. "And there's never been a sycophant like you."

The sound of more concrete flowing down upon them made it hard to hear.

"Um," Clover asked anxiously, "is this where we're supposed to end up? I mean, is this how it ends?"

Geth remained quiet as he tried to right his thoughts and feelings.

"I'm going to take that as a no," Clover said, relieved. "Because there's always hope, right?"

Geth was too heartbroken to reply.

"Well, I'll answer that for you," Clover said firmly. "Yes. And I can tell you right now there's no way I'm not getting back to Lilly and Leven."

Geth stared into the darkness as the concrete continued to pour. He gripped his hands together and closed his eyes as his soul experienced a large dose of despair for the first time in his life.

"Yep," Clover said assuredly. "There's always hope."

Clover patted Geth on the head and then held onto his neck.

Fate was playing dirty.

## ◆ Epilogue ◆

# URGENCY

Winter marched into the stone hall with purpose. Her long blonde hair was straight and beautiful and her green eyes looked like dark bits of a mystery that no man could ever solve. She was thin and almost as fetching as Phoebe, who was walking next to her. Phoebe had the added advantage of being a longing, a breed that naturally made all those she came in contact with dazed and confused.

"We have something," Winter said with conviction.

Leven turned and faced them. Having just returned from searching Cusp, he was tired and worried. It had been over a week since they had heard anything from Geth or Clover, and they were beginning to feel real concern. There had been much searching, but no sign of them anywhere. Lilly was sick, Phoebe was beside herself, and Winter was having a hard time acting confident about anything.

"What'd you find?" Leven asked hopefully.

"There was a dead onus found in the bottom of Stone Canyon," Winter said, stepping close to Leven. "It's been dead at least a week."

Leven looked into her green eyes, and his eyes burned gold.

"And we found this," Winter said, holding up a muddy shirt. "It's Geth's."

Leven smiled.

"This might be bad," Winter said, surprised by Leven's expression.

"Did you find anything else?" Leven said with excitement.

"No," Phoebe answered sadly, her eyes tired from holding back her tears. "Just a dead onus and Geth's shirt. There were some footprints leading off, but the ground has been washed over and it's hard to tell."

"That canyon runs next to the Hidden Border, right?" Leven asked.

"It does," Winter answered, curious about Leven's sudden excitement.

"That would explain the dreams I've been having," Leven almost cheered. "We need to leave immediately."

"You have millions of dreams," Winter reminded him. "You're the Want."

"These dreams were different," Leven said, taking Winter's hand. "Let's go."

"We'll need Lilly," Winter insisted.

"Of course," Leven agreed.

The three of them walked swiftly from the room and out into the air of Foo.